TROUBLE AT THE REDSTONE

John D. Nesbitt

LEISURE BOOKS NEW YORK CITY

For Dave Manning

A LEISURE BOOK®

October 2008

Published by

Dorchester Publishing Co., Inc.
200 Madison Avenue
New York, NY 10016

ISBN 10: 0-8439-6055-8
ISBN 13: 978-0-8439-6055-6

Printed in the United States of America.

10 9 8 7 6 5 4 3 2 1

Visit us on the web at www.dorchesterpub.com.

ITCHING FOR A FIGHT

"How about it?" said the surly man in chaps.

"Mr. Aden, I don't know what you're gettin' at," Will said.

"Just Aden to you. Don't mister me."

"Good enough."

Aden was standing up straight now. "Well, how about it?"

"How about what?"

"Are you a good hand with a mop stick?"

Will frowned and looked away, then turned and said, "I wonder if there's somethin' eatin' on you."

Aden took a drink of his whiskey and set the glass down on the bar with a thump. "I don't like drifters."

"Well, you don't have to, even if I was one."

"Even if you were one." Aden sneered. "You've got it written all over you. I know your type."

Will's blood was rising, "You know a lot."

"Enough to get by. And enough to take care of myself."

Here it comes, Will thought. *Look out...*

Trouble at the Redstone

Chapter One

Will Dryden stood up from his cot as the jailer came toward his cell, jingling his large ring of keys. At Dryden's cell he stopped, shook a key loose from the bunch, and clacked it into the lock. Then he pushed the door open and stepped aside.

"Time to go."

"Go where?" Will thought he had seen the last of the judge and it was just a matter of sitting out his ten days.

"Just go." The slender man motioned with his bald head toward the front of the jail and let the prisoner go first.

Will passed through the heavy door and stopped in the office, where he saw his hat, his pocketknife, a few coins, his spurs, and his gun and holster on the sheriff's desk. The sheriff himself was nowhere to be seen.

The jailer went behind the desk, put the key ring in the top drawer, and then with a smaller key locked the desk. "You can go now."

"What gives? I've got six days left to do."

The jailer shook his head and handed Will a folded slip of paper.

Will opened it and saw, in a neat cursive hand, a short message.

Ask for Mrs. Irma Welles at the Northwestern Hotel.

He raised his eyes and found the jailer watching him. "Did this person pay my bail?"

"Paid off the rest of your fine."

"Right." Will put the note in his vest pocket with his cigarette makin's, then reached for his hat and put it on. He scooped up the change—thirty-seven cents—and dropped it into his trouser pocket, followed by his pocketknife. As he reached for his spurs and six-gun, he asked, "Where's my belt?"

"Didn't have one."

"Of course I had a belt, else I wouldn't have been able to wear this."

"I don't know." The jailer turned away, opened a cabinet door, and peered inside. "Maybe it's this," he said, drawing out a belt and holding it at arm's length like a dangling snake.

"That's it." Will put on the belt and holster, picked up his spurs, and paused. "Thanks," he said.

"All the same."

He walked out into the bright day and found a bench to sit on, two doors down. There he buckled on his spurs and sat back to roll and smoke a cigarette. As he looked up and down the street, he saw the sign for the Northwestern Hotel about a block away. This was a strange deal, he thought. Someone getting him out of the pokey, and now just sitting here, he could get up and walk away if he wanted. But that didn't seem right. He looked at the note again. Whoever this Mrs. Welles was, he figured he owed it to her to at least thank her and find out what she wanted. But the last part was what kept him from being in a hurry. A woman didn't pay off an unknown man's jail time out of charity.

As Will stood at the desk and waited for the hotel clerk to go for Mrs. Welles, he had a pretty good sense of what he looked like—a man who had been in the same clothes day and night for a week and who needed a bath and a shave. But at least he was sober and well rested.

After a few minutes the clerk came down the stairway, followed by a woman of everyday appearance. She wore a long, pale blue dress with a lightweight jacket of darker blue. Her light hair, somewhere between brown and blonde, was tied up and around in back. She would not have turned his head on the street, but she was not unpleasant to look at.

As she reached the bottom of the stairs and came forward, he turned, hat in hand, and waited for her. Now he saw her bluish gray eyes and a few hard lines in her face. He also caught a glance of her rising bosom beneath the dark blue jacket, but he made himself look again at her facial features. He figured her to be about his age or a little more, maybe in her early thirties.

"I'm Mrs. Welles," she said, holding out her hand.

"Will Dryden." He took her hand and released it, noticing that it was not a hand rough from work but not a soft lady's hand either.

"Shall we sit down?" She motioned to a pair of wooden armchairs on the far side of the lobby, up against a wall that had no windows but a silent, staring mule deer head with a broad spread of antlers.

He followed her and took a seat after she did, setting his chair so that it faced hers at an angle.

"Thank you for coming," she began.

"Thank you," he answered, "for getting me out of that place. A few days was more than enough."

She gave a light laugh. "Well, I'm glad to be able to do something that makes another person's life more bearable." She paused, then added, "But I admit it was not a pure act of philanthropy."

"I wouldn't expect it."

Her hands moved in her lap, and he saw that she was holding a small purse. He raised his glance to meet hers.

She took a breath and began in a deliberate tone, as if she had thought out her words ahead of time. "The case is, Mr. Dryden, that I have a little bit of work that I need done."

He met her steady eyes. "People often do."

"And I'm wondering if you might be interested."

"Depends on what it is. If it's something that would get me in trouble, I'd just as soon be back over there, eatin' boiled cabbage and workin' off my fine myself."

"Oh, of course. And don't get me wrong. I don't expect you to take this job just because I paid your fine. I did that much so we could have this conversation. Any future work would have its own compensation."

He forced himself to keep his eyes matched with hers, yet at the lower edge of his vision he could see her hands and the purse. "It's good of you to state things outright like that."

"I think it's good to have things clear and straight from the beginning." She smiled without showing her teeth.

"So do I." He waited for her to speak, and when she didn't, he said, "Go ahead. I'm willing to hear what you've got in mind."

The woman drew a breath as before, and her chest rose a little. "Mr. Dryden, my husband has gone missing, and I need someone to try to find him."

Will let his gaze rove across her face, which showed no expression. "Do you think he's here in Enfield, or somewhere near?"

She shook her head. "No, I don't think so. The best information I have is that he was last seen in Thorne. Do you know that town?"

"I know of it. It's about a day's ride west of here."

"That's right." She gave a small nod.

Will reflected for a moment. "Did you have someone else looking for him before?"

"No. I found out that much myself. But I didn't think it seemed proper for a woman to go any further looking for her husband."

"Depends on where he went, I suppose."

Her face softened. "Mr. Dryden, I realize it appears as if I'm just a woman whose husband has run out on her, and that may turn out to be the case." Her hand went up to brush away the hair at her temple, and then it returned to its proper pose on her lap. "But I think something might have happened to him. If it did, I would want to know."

"Of course." Will had the impression that if she came to know the worst, it would not devastate her. "Tell me, Mrs. Welles, what your husband's first name is."

She looked down at her lap and then at Will. "Actually, the name isn't Welles. It's just a name I've been using for purposes of discretion."

"I see."

"His name is Alfred Vetch. He goes by Al."

"That's good to know."

"And, just to put all my cards on the table, I can tell you that my name is Elinore, not Irma. But I'll keep the name of Irma Welles for as long as I'm on this venture, so if you agree to do this piece of work for me, that would be the name I would travel under and would use for correspondence, just as I have done."

"That's understandable."

"And agreeable?" She gave him what he took to be an appraising look.

"No reason I should object. Or do you mean the job as well?"

"Mr. Dryden, I need someone to carry out this task."

Will paused for a few seconds, then said, "Just to find Al Vetch, not to bring him back with his hands tied to a saddle horn?"

She smiled and showed her teeth, which were clean and even. "Just to find him. Once I know where he is, and under what circumstances, I can decide what I should do."

Silence hung in the air, and he knew she was waiting for an answer. "I suppose so. But to give me an idea of what I might be getting into—"

"Go ahead."

"Has Mr. Vetch had the tendency to get mixed up in any shady dealings?"

"Such as?"

"Little things in the dark, usually for easy money."

"Oh, no. He wouldn't ever do anything like that."

Will thought her answer came too quick, but it told him as much as he was likely to learn at the moment.

"Well, even if he did, all I have to do is find him. I was just wondering whether to look in broad daylight or in darker places."

She gave her open smile again. "I think you're worldly-wise enough to know not to overlook any possibilities."

"But I probably won't find him minding a town herd of milk cows, or tending the coal chute at a train station."

She had a droll expression as she shook her head. "Probably not."

Will reflected again. "You said a few minutes ago that you thought something might have happened to him."

Her answer was quick and short. "It was just a feeling."

"I understand." Another question took form. "Did, or does, he have a life insurance policy?"

"Not that I know of."

"Just a thought."

She sat up straight, shifting in her seat, and then smiled at him. "So tell me, Mr. Dryden, how you ended up in that disagreeable place." She motioned with her head in the general direction of the jail.

"Well, as I imagine you know, it was for disturbing the peace."

"Of course I know that. But what did you do to get there?"

He tipped his head to one side. "I don't remember very well, but from the bumps and bruises I ended up with, I believe I must have disturbed some individual's peace."

She gave a light laugh. "Go on."

He figured she already knew the general details and on the basis of that she decided he might be a good man for the job she had in mind. But he had no reason for playing coy, so he went on as she asked him to. "It was a fight, of course. I don't remember the particulars, though I played it through my mind a thousand times while I was soakin' in the jail. I was playing cards, and there was a fellow across the table who seemed to take a dislike to me." A blurred image came floating up, and Will shook it away. "I don't know why. Then at some point, someone must have slipped something into my drink, because the next thing I remember, I was lying on the floor getting kicked in the head and ribs."

Her face was thoughtful as she nodded.

"I woke up in jail, and of course my money was all gone and I had nothing to pay my bail with. Same thing when I went before the judge, so he gave me ten days. I was sittin' it out when you came along."

She seemed to be giving him another appraisal. "Well, all I heard was that you were a man who probably knew how to take care of himself but ran into some bad luck."

"I did that." He met her eyes. "And I thank you again for getting me out."

Her eyes had a bit of sparkle as she said, "All for the purpose of having this conversation."

"Good enough. I suppose we're in agreement."

She raised her hand about chest high. "There's the matter of payment. What would you say to my giving you fifty dollars now, another fifty when you're done, and something on top of that if it takes more than a month?"

Will took a minute to think it through. As he understood it, the better detective agencies charged by the day, plus travel expenses. A flat fee might encourage an operative to arrive at conclusions too quickly. On the other hand, reputable agencies didn't take on cases that entailed gathering evidence that might lead to a divorce suit, which this case looked like, at least on the surface. This woman had no doubt considered the options, might even have talked to a seedy detective or two, and had decided to try things this way. Will figured Al Vetch was either living with another woman behind drawn curtains or was lying facedown at the bottom of a mine somewhere. Even if he was off doing crooked work, like forging deeds or selling shares on a bogus company, Will should know within a month whether the man was to be found.

"What if, after a month, I decide I can't find this fellow?"

"That's fine. You get your month's pay regardless."

After a few seconds he said, "All right. That sounds fair."

"Good." She sat poised. "Is there anything we haven't covered?"

"Maybe a couple of things, Mrs. Welles—if that's the name we're using between us."

She smiled and nodded. "Oh, yes."

"I was wondering if you had a picture of this man."

Her face clouded. "No, I don't. I wish I did, especially for this purpose."

"Can you tell me what he looks like?"

She tipped her head and made a little shrug.

"He's an average-looking sort of man—average height and build. He's thirty-five years old. Brown hair, brown eyes."

"Beard? Mustache? Balding hair?"

She shook her head. "None of that."

"How does he dress? What kind of work has he done?"

Her eyebrows raised. "He usually works in a business—hardware, freighting."

"Office work, then. Not a miner or cowpuncher, for example."

"Oh, no. In fact, he's done some land-office work."

"Do you think he's in one of those lines of work right now?"

"I don't know. He always complains that he's not making enough money."

"Does he go armed?"

"When he travels, yes. Sometimes he travels for his work."

"Uh-huh. By the way, when you went, um, looking for him, did you ask for him by name?"

"Yes, I did. Why?"

"Well, I figure I'd better not do the same, right away. I might have to go about it in a roundabout way."

"Whatever you think is best."

Will studied her face. She kept up a strong, expressionless front when she wanted. "I guess I have one more question," he said.

"Very well."

"Deep down, what do you think he's doing?"

"You want to know what I really think?"

"Sure."

She raised her chin as she took a breath. "I think he's trying to raise some money so he can go somewhere else."

"Yet you said he wouldn't do anything shady."

She smiled. "Oh, Mr. Dryden, it was quite a bit earlier in the conversation when I said that. I think we understand each other better now."

"Well, you did tell me not to overlook any possibilities."

Her eyes sparkled. "Yes, I did."

The first few dollars of his operating money went fast. After asking around, he found his horse and paid the stable bill. Then he went to the barbershop, where he had a shave and a bath. Wearing his wrinkled but clean change of clothes from his duffel bag, he found a washwoman to take care of the clothes he had been living in. She told him she would have them washed, dried, and folded before sundown. As it was now about two in the afternoon, he went to a café and ordered a meal of steak and potatoes. That, and a mug of cool beer, made the world seem like not such a bad place.

From the pleasant smile on the waitress's face, he could tell he looked quite a bit more presentable than he had when he was sitting beneath the deer head with Mrs. Welles. In spite of his shabby appearance, though, he thought she had given him a good looking-over and had not found him repulsive. In spite of her reserve, and her role as the concerned wife, he thought she would look at him with even more interest now that he was scrubbed and clean.

He told himself it didn't matter. She was paying

him to do a job, and he needed to keep his mind straight for that. Come sundown, he needed to put this town behind him and get out on the trail to Thorne.

Chapter Two

Will rested his horse at the top of a rise. He dismounted, and as he rolled and smoked a cigarette, he took in the country around him. It was still grassland but had become more broken, with dry-wash gullies fingering off in all directions. The grass had become poorer, too, with bare spots of a hand's width between clumps. Prickly pear cactus grew in low, broad clumps, and stirrup-high sagebrush dotted the hills and gullies everywhere. He had passed a couple of large alkali flats, so even the cactus and sagebrush looked hospitable by comparison.

He tipped back his hat and dragged his shirtsleeve across his forehead. His mouth was dry, but he didn't want to drink the last pint of water in his canteen while he could still resist. He had gotten in a couple of hours of travel the night before and then had made an early start this morning, so he ought to make the town of Thorne by late afternoon. If he found water for his horse before then, so much the better.

Down off the hill he rode. When the trail leveled out, a jackrabbit broke from the cover of a clump of sagebrush. The animal took off at a run, veering one way and then another but generally keeping a straightaway course, with the black tips of his ears aloft like deer horns. Will knew that if he whistled a bullet that way, the jackrabbit could put on a hell of a lot more speed. It was tempting, but there was no sense in making noise and wasting ammunition.

A mile later he passed a prairie dog town on his left, a colony of burrows that covered nearly ten acres. The bare dirt shone pale in the sun, and here and there a tawny little rodent poked his head up out of a hole. Again, Will felt the temptation to take some target practice, but he let common sense prevail.

A few miles farther, a way station came into view. It sat back from the trail about fifty yards, against the backdrop of a low ridge. Will imagined that the shadows of late afternoon and early evening would give some benefit, and he supposed that the ridge helped to blunt some of the winter winds that blew out of that quarter.

The station itself was a typical structure, with walls of sod. Roof poles jutted out in front, and on each side of the solid plank door, a small window sat high in the wall. A set of patched-together corrals lay off to the right and farther back. To the left, a small area about twenty feet square was enclosed by a rail fence and no gate. It did not look like a corral, and as Will drew his horse to a stop at the hitching rail, he stood in his stirrups for a better view. He thought it might be an oil seep.

As he swung down from the saddle, the front door of the building opened and a human form appeared. The man lingered in the shadowy doorway, and his presence suggested a smudgy quality.

"Good afternoon," said Will.

"Same to you."

Will cast a light glance across the front of the building. "What place is this?"

"Dunn Station."

"I see."

The man took a step forward, and Will got a better view of him. He was not a hulking type, but his body had thickened in middle age, and his sagging paunch hung out between his suspenders. He had a full head of short brown hair, and a stubbled beard of the same color. His dark eyes moved from Will to the horse and back.

"Suppose you want some water."

"If I could. Just a little to begin with. Couple of gallons."

The man went inside and came out wearing a dark-stained brown hat. "Trough's around back."

Will led the horse as he followed the man to the rear of the building. There he loosened the cinch and let the horse drink a few long swallows. He filled his canteen at the pump, got a drink for himself, and rinsed his hands and face. Then he led the horse back to the rail in front and tied him there.

All this time, the proprietor watched without saying anything. Then when the horse was tied, he asked, "Where ya headed?"

"Town called Thorne."

The man gave a knowing nod. "A few miles further on." He looked Will up and down and said, "Lookin' fer work?"

"About the only thing worth lookin' for that won't get a man in trouble."

"Isn't that right?" The man's heavy brows went up a little. "Anything else I can git for you today?"

Will glanced past him toward the door. "I wouldn't mind sittin' down for a few minutes, let my horse soak up what he drank before I give him another slug."

"Sure, come on in. We can chin a while."

Will followed him into the dim establishment, which was lit only by the light coming in from the two windows and the open door. As his eyes adjusted, he could see it was a typical roadhouse, with a bar and two tables at the tavern end and a store counter at the end where goods were sold. The center area was taken up by shelves and a long, narrow table. At a glance Will could see canned goods, sacks of dry food such as flour and beans, and odds and ends of rope, chain, leather, and burlap.

The proprietor took a seat at one of the two tables near the bar. He did not take off his hat, so Will didn't bother to, either. When they were both seated, the man folded his arms across his stomach and said, "Lookin' fer work. What kind do you do?"

"Mostly ranch work, but I've done my share of other things. Not too fond of lumberjackin' or underground minin'. Or sheepherdin'."

"Me neither."

"And I don't think I could make a livin' shoein' mules."

"Huh. Them that wants it can have it."

"That's what I say. By the way, my name's Will Dryden." He held out his hand.

"Orry Dunn. No one bothers with the first name. I don't."

"Good enough," said Will as they shook. After a few seconds he said, "I wonder if there's much work around here."

"Well, there's sheep in this country, but you say you don't care for that."

"Not if I can find something more to my likin'."

Dunn pushed out his cheek with his tongue and

said, "Well, there's one ranch out south of Thorne, they run cattle, and they might need a hand."

"Is that right? What's the name of the place?"

"It's called the Redstone. Owner's a fella named Donovan, mucky-muck type, but his foreman does the hirin' and firin'."

"That's good enough."

"Foreman's name is Ingram. Earl Ingram."

"Have you got any idea what kind of outfit it is to work for?"

Dunn shrugged. "Pretty regular most of the time, from what I've heard."

"Most of the time?"

"Well, I think the reason they might need a hand right now is that one of their riders got killed a few days ago."

"Really? Did he take a spill on a horse?"

"No, it was a bullet."

"Gunfight?"

"Nope. He was just out ridin', as the story goes, and someone put a hole in him. Young feller, pretty easygoin' as I knew him, and not the kind to pick any quarrel with anyone."

"Huh. That's too bad."

"It is." After a few seconds of silence, Dunn spoke again. "Say, are you sure there's not anything I can get for you?"

Will thought for a second. "Why not? Have you got any beer?"

"I do. It's not ice-cold, but the keg hasn't been open very long, so it tastes right."

Will raised his chin. "I'd go for a glass of it. And I'd be happy to invite you to have one with me."

"I'm not in the habit of turnin' it down." Dunn

pushed back his chair and stood up. "I'll be right back."

He returned with two glasses of beer, not frosty but with a half inch of foam on top. "Here you go," he said, setting them on the table.

When the proprietor was seated, Will raised his glass and touched it to the other man's. As Dunn had said, the beer was not cold but it had a good bite to it.

"Glad to find a product like this on hand."

Dunn smacked his lips. "It's like other things. When a man knows where to git it, that's where he goes."

"I believe you're right." Will took another drink, smaller this time. "How long have you been here at this place?"

"A little under ten years."

"Does well enough, then."

"I get by."

Will brought out the makin's and went about rolling a cigarette. After he lit it, he said, "That looked like an oil seep out there."

"That's what it is."

Will blew out a stream of smoke. "Do you get much good out of it?"

Dunn turned down the corners of his mouth. "Oh, some. Wagons and such."

"Do you make axle grease out of it?"

"That's right. Thicken it with flour or corn starch."

Will nodded. He figured that was where some of the smudges on the man's clothes might have come from. "Mostly freighters?"

"Them, and just people movin' from one place to another."

"Emigrants."

"Uh-huh."

"Good idea to keep it fenced."

"Oh, yeah. It could be a hell of a nuisance."

Will took another drink. "Do the sheepherders come in for this stuff?"

"Oh, some do, but not as much as the cowpunchers. Them sheepherders, you know, they're tied down to their sheep. Kind of a queer bunch sometimes. They live alone for months at a time, maybe keep a jug of wine or a stash of whiskey, but get along on next to nothin'."

"They can be solitary, all right." Will took a drag on his cigarette.

"Fools, too. I knew one, come winter, he'd go into Rawlins and moon over a whore, same one every year, spend all his wages on her and whiskey, and then go back to the sheep wagon, flat-ass broke and nothin' to show for it."

"Some of 'em don't even care for women."

"They're probably better suited to that kind of work."

"Each man to his poison. Me, I like to go into town once in a while and see if there's any petticoats to rustle."

Dunn set down his glass, empty now, and smacked his lips again. "Been known to do that myself. Not as much as when I was your age, but sometimes it happens."

"What kind of places have they got in Thorne?"

"They don't have a whorehouse, if that's what you mean. But they've got a couple of saloons and then all the normal stuff. Store, hotel, stable, blacksmith shop." Dunn shrugged. "Nothin' new." He took out a tobacco pouch, and with his thumb and first two fingers lifted a stringy wad and tucked it into his left cheek.

"Good place to start, though, I guess."

"I'd say. If you can't find anything else, and if you're not superstitious, you can try gettin' on at the Redstone."

Will smiled. "Shall I tell them you recommended it?"

Dunn spit out a fleck of tobacco with the tip of his tongue. "Oh, I don't think Ingram would care. But the big boss, Donovan, I don't believe he would be impressed."

"Oh."

"He likes people to kiss his ass, and I don't do that. I'm more likely to say what I think." He picked up a can from the floor and spit into it. " 'Course, maybe that's why I'm here and he's there. And that's all right, too."

The town of Thorne looked normal enough, with all the businesses lined along the Main Street. Houses were scattered out behind on each side, with plenty of vacant lots among them. Here and there a bottle on a rubbish heap caught the late-afternoon rays of the sun. Smoke rose from a few stovepipes, so Will imagined some households were getting started on the evening meal. He heard a couple of dogs barking, but he did not see any women or children.

The first saloon he came to was called the Lucky Diamond. The sign had a picture of a gemstone, balanced upright on a point like a child's top, with flat tapering sides and a crown with a dozen facets. Figuring that one saloon was as good as another, Will swung down and tied his horse. He heard men's voices inside as he stepped onto the sidewalk and moved toward the door.

Inside, the place had not yet been lit up for the

evening, but a lamp above each end of the bar kept it from being as dim as Dunn's place. A few men stood along the bar, while behind it, on a stool, sat a man who could pass for a brother of the jailer in Enfield.

Will called for a beer and took a glance at the other patrons, who looked like the regular run of working men. He laid a silver dollar on the counter, which the bartender acknowledged as he set down the beer.

The first man down the bar had his back to Will. He wore the outfit of a range rider, including chaps, which not all of the riders on the northern ranges wore at this time of year. He also had the handle of a six-gun hanging out in view. Will had already decided not to ask for Al Vetch at all and not to mention the Redstone right away, but rather to find out what any of these men might have to offer.

After a few minutes, the man in the chaps turned, and Will got a full view of him. As a physical type, he looked like other men Will had known—slender and not very tall, hook-nosed and deep-eyed. He had light brown hair visible below a large-brimmed, mouse-colored hat. His face was clean shaven, and he no doubt put some stock in his appearance, for he had a large red handkerchief loose around his neck and tied in a thick knot. He wore a denim jacket, open in front, and beneath that a red cotton shirt. With two breast pockets and a row of buttons all the way down, the shirt would cost nearly twice the price of a common work shirt. Hanging out beneath the flap of the left pocket was the yellow string and circular tab of a sack of Bull Durham. The man also had a lit cigarette in his left hand, which he rested on the bar near a glass of whiskey. His right hand hung by its thumb at the top of his chaps, not far from the pistol handle.

After a few seconds, Will said, "Good afternoon."

"Same to you." The man moved the cigarette to his mouth and pulled in a lungful.

"Time of day when a drink goes good."

The other man puffed out a cloud of smoke and let it drift upward in front of him. "Which way'd you come in?"

Will adjusted to the question. "From the east."

"All the way from Cheyenne?"

"Not recently."

With the cigarette between his fingers, the man lifted his glass and tossed off the rest of his whiskey. "People come from every direction. Most of the time, they're not goin' to any place better."

Will noted a Southern accent by now. "Might be. Sometimes they're lookin' for opportunity, and sometimes they just want a better climate."

"Anyone who'd come here for the climate has got the brains of a sheep."

"Oh, there's more than one kind of climate."

"Meanin'?"

"Some folks come west to get away from the fever and muggy weather, some go south to get away from the cold, and some go just about anywhere to get away from the hot water."

"Plenty of them." The man cast a glance over Will, as if to suggest he might be one of the latter. Then he said, "How far west you headed? You know the whole country's drier'n hell right now."

Will took a sip of his beer. "Heard that. I don't have a real destination, though. I've been stoppin' in each town to see what kind of work there might be."

"Not much. I can tell you that."

"Oh, it doesn't take much. Not for just one man. Work a while, maybe for the season."

The bartender appeared with a bottle. "Another one, Max?"

"Sure." As the bartender filled the glass, Max took a last pull on his cigarette, dropped it on the floor, and ground it out with his spurred boot. Then he turned his unfriendly eyes on Will again. "Last I heard, the most work was in Idaho. A couple of big mines are goin' at it."

"Something to remember."

" 'Course it's hard work, and some fellas don't like that."

"Work's work."

"Somethin' to talk about, for a lot of men."

Will was picking up a note of antagonism. "How's that?"

"They talk about work more than they do it. Work a couple of days, drift for a month."

"I guess some are like that."

"You guess."

Will turned to his drink and didn't answer.

"You don't look like you've been worn down too much by work."

"Maybe I handle it well."

"Handle what? A mop stick, a pitchfork?"

A shaft of light entered the saloon as two cow-punchers came in through the door. Will took advantage of the distraction and kept to himself.

One of the punchers walked over to Max, clapped him on the shoulder, and said, "Well if it ain't Max Aden. What are you up to?"

Max shrugged away the man's hand. "Same as always."

The puncher looked at Will and said, "Makin' friends, huh?" Then he and his partner walked farther down the bar.

"How about it?" said the surly man in chaps.

"Mr. Aden, I don't know what you're gettin' at."

"Just Aden to you. Don't mister me."

"Good enough."

Aden was standing up straight now. "Well, how about it?"

"How about what?"

"Are you a good hand with a mop stick?"

Will frowned and looked away, then turned and said, "I wonder if there's somethin' eatin' on you."

Aden took a drink of his whiskey and set the glass down with a thump. "I don't like drifters."

"Well, you don't have to, even if I was one."

"Even if you were one." Aden sneered. "You've got it written all over you. Sleep in the stable, shit in the corner and cover it with straw. I know your type."

Will's blood was rising. "You know a lot."

"Enough to get by. And enough to take care of myself."

Here it comes, Will thought. *Look out.*

"Don't sit there like a dummy. I'm talkin' to you."

Will faced him square. "Look here, fella. I don't know what's got into you, or why you think you need to get so cheeky with me. But you're not gonna get me to go for my gun. Not over something as petty as this."

Aden lifted his head and scowled. "Who said anything about that? I can clean your plow with my two hands."

Will took a deep breath. "Put your gun on the bar, then, and I'll do the same. Then we'll see about it."

Aden stood tense, his face reddening, and then his body relaxed as he unbuckled his gun belt and chaps, set them on the bar, and put his jacket and hat on top.

Will did the same with his own gun and hat, and

the two men moved away from the bar and put up their fists.

Stripped down for fighting, and with a receding hairline more visible, Aden looked smaller than before, but Will knew that men his size could be dangerous—especially if they were out to prove themselves, as this one seemed to be.

The two men moved back and forth, shifting their feet but not throwing a punch. After a half minute or so, Aden stood still and lowered his guard. Beckoning with his open right hand, he said, "Come on, saddle tramp. Don't be afraid."

Will stepped forward to give him a jab, and the little man came back with a left and a right—good, solid blows to each side of Will's face. Then the man was out and away.

Will moved toward him, faking with his left and then crossing with his right. Aden took the punch by turning his head aside, and with a continued motion he lowered his head, moved forward, and came up swinging. Will blocked the left punch but caught the right one full on his jaw.

Both men backed off to regroup. Aden brought up his guard and moved to his left. Will did the same. Then with a flurry the other man lunged forward, swinging left-right, left-right. The punches stung like huge hailstones, but they didn't have a great deal of shock.

Will stepped back, and Aden came at him again. This time Will took advantage of his opponent's forward motion, as he planted his foot and leaned into a right cross. He connected square on Aden's cheekbone and rocked him back onto his heels. He kept moving forward, landing a left that glanced off and then a right that sent Aden staggering backward.

The little man caught his balance and came up into position. Will held up, and the two of them went back into circling.

Now Aden rushed again, this time getting in close and dropping his shoulder into Will's abdomen. Will brought his right elbow down on the man's head, but not before Aden got the toe of his boot onto Will's spur and pushed him over backward.

Aden hit the floor as well, then reared back, seething, and smashed a fist into Will's face. Will bucked to one side, and the two of them went flailing and thrashing. Will found himself wedged up against the brass foot rail of the bar, and then Aden was on his feet, pushing a boot into Will's chest. The hat and chaps fell off the bar, and Will thought, *He's going for his gun.*

The thought gave him a charge of energy. He grabbed the shank of the boot, put his left hand on the toe, and turned the foot. Aden straightened up, hopped on his left foot, then spilled onto the floor. Will came up on his hands and knees and pushed forward in a lunge.

Aden was on his feet again, with the chaps in his left hand. He stepped back and brought the leather down with a heavy slap on the back of Will's head.

It almost sent him to the floor, but he pushed up and surprised Aden with a solid left punch to the jaw, followed by a right uppercut. Aden dropped the chaps and stepped back, his guard still down. Will moved in and gave him two more, at which the man staggered to the bar and leaned there. His gun belt was within reach, but he didn't make a move for it.

"That's enough," said the bartender, who stood with a single-barreled shotgun leveled across the bar.

Will studied the man. As long as Aden was holding his own or better, the bartender had let the fight go on. Then when the tide turned, he brought out his scattergun.

"Mister," he said, without pointing the weapon at Will, "we don't like trouble in here."

Will took a second to answer. "Neither do I, but he started ridin' me from the minute he saw me. If this is the only fight he ever picked in here, I'd be surprised."

"Max just doesn't take much guff. I suppose you know that by now."

"He gives out plenty to begin with."

"Look here, mister. Don't try startin' things all over again."

Will looked at Aden and then back at the bartender. "Farthest thing from my mind. I've had enough, and I'd guess he has, too."

Aden had pulled himself together enough to muster up a full look of resentment. "I'd say you should have enough. But I'll tell you this. Next time you want to get thumped, look me up. I'm not hard to find."

Will glanced at the chaps on the floor. "Sure. We'll have a fair fight. Just you and anything you can get your hands on."

Aden stood with his fists clenched at his side. "You can find out what I can do with my two hands."

"Don't count on it. You can find someone else to prove yourself with." Will moved to the bar, picked up his gun and holster with his left hand, and pushed the silver dollar toward the bartender. Then he put on his hat and walked to the door.

Outside, he saw there was still enough daylight to find the Redstone Ranch and ask about a job. Even if they didn't need anyone, he would be welcome to spend the night. That would be better than another night on the hard ground.

As he gathered his reins and led the horse into the street, he said, half to himself and half to his horse, "Next time I want to get thumped. To hell with that fella. All I want is to do what I set out to do." He put his foot in the stirrup, swung aboard, and put the Lucky Diamond behind him.

Chapter Three

Will found the Redstone without any trouble after asking two separate people in town. He rode into the ranch yard just as the sun was slipping behind the hills—a few minutes before nine in the evening, according to his pocket watch.

The headquarters were laid out in a familiar pattern. A barn of unpainted lumber sat on his left as he rode in, and attached to the east side of it ran a stable with a lower roof. Behind lay a set of corrals, with a pasture stretching away to the south on the far side of the corrals. Straight ahead of him sat the main building, which he took to be the ranch house. It was a two-story building made of quarried stone, with a set of stone steps leading up to the front porch. Off to the left of the house, near the back corner, sat a smaller structure of matching stone. Will supposed it was a springhouse. On the right flank of the ranch yard Will observed two wooden buildings. The smaller one might be either the cookshack or the foreman's house, while the other, longer one was no doubt a bunkhouse.

The ranch yard itself was dry and hard-packed now in midsummer, and the hooves of Will's horse gave out a *tlock-tlock, tlock-tlock* sound that carried on the cool evening air. A man appeared at the bunkhouse door and stepped outside. He was wearing typical ranch clothes, including a hat and a vest, and he was picking his teeth with a toothpick.

Will turned his horse toward the bunkhouse and came to a stop at the hitching rail. As he dismounted and stepped into view, the man came forward and spoke out.

"Good evening."

"Good evening to you."

"Anything I can help you with?"

"I was hopin' to find the foreman."

The man gave a faint smile, and his mustache lifted. "Well, you've done that."

"That's good." Will paused for a couple of seconds and said, "I was wonderin' if you were lookin' to put on any more help."

The foreman poked the toothpick into the corner of his mouth. "Might could." He looked Will over. "You a regular hand?"

"Oh, yeah."

"Well, we finished roundup just a few days ago, so we'll be doin' the usual range work. Ride out from here most of the time, sometimes pack an outfit and set out for a couple of days. Dependin'."

"Sure."

"Pay's a dollar a day and found."

"Sounds fine."

The foreman motioned with his head toward the other building. "That's the cookshack. Supper's long over, but there might be somethin' left."

"I'm all right."

"Good enough." The man glanced at Will's outfit. "You can leave your saddle in the barn, you'll find a rack, and put your horse in the pasture out back. You'll be ridin' company horses. Then when you get that done, you can bring your gear into the bunkhouse."

The foreman's eyes came back to Will. "By the way, what's your name?"

"Will Dryden."

"Good to know you. I'm Earl Ingram." The two men shook.

With only one lamp glowing in the bunkhouse, Will did not see everything at once as he stepped inside. He paused with his duffel bag in one hand and his bedroll in the other.

Ingram, no longer wearing a hat, rose from his chair. "There's a couple of empty bunks," he said. "You can have your pick."

Will noticed the man's full head of sandy brown hair, his blue eyes, full mustache, and solid facial features. He was probably close to forty, but he held his age well, and he carried an air of easy authority.

"Thanks." Will looked around to see another man, about the same age as the foreman and also hatless, sitting at a square table. He was smoking a curved-stem pipe and fiddling with a deck of cards.

The man took the pipe out of his mouth and said, "Evenin'. I'm Jim."

"Howdy. I'm Will."

Jim smiled. "Pleased to meet you. Let me know if I can help."

"Thanks." Will looked off to the right and saw a younger, dark-haired man sitting on the edge of his bunk.

"There's Brad," said Jim.

The young puncher and Will exchanged greetings.

"And over there's Max." Jim pointed with his pipe to the next cot beyond Brad's.

At the edge of the dim light, a man in a red shirt

lay with his back to the rest of the men. On the wall near his bunk hung a pair of chaps.

The man rolled over and sat up, and Will had no doubt as to who he was. The sullen, deep-set eyes belonged to Max Aden.

"We met earlier," he said, not looking at Will. "He's the bum from the Lucky Diamond."

Jim took a puff on his pipe. "He seems to have gotten back on his feet pretty quickly."

"Well, I'll knock him down the first time he gives me any talk."

The foreman's voice came up. "Now look here, Max. You know damn well there's not goin' to be any fightin' here. If there is, you'll both go packin'."

"Yeah, yeah. But mark my words. He's trouble."

Jim spoke again. "No need to stand there all night with your gear, fella. Let's get you a bunk. You can have the one next to Max, or you can have the one on the other side of mine. It was Ben's, the fella who's not with us anymore. We can move those things that are on it."

Will let out his breath. "That would be just as well."

Jim rose from his seat, laid his pipe on the table, and walked to the bunk in question. He picked up the most prominent item, a black hat with a round peak and curled brim, and set it on his head. Then he gathered up the four corners of the gray wool blanket, reached under the bunk to draw out a canvas bag, and transferred all the belongings to the bunk next to Aden's.

"Go ahead," he called over his shoulder.

Will set his bag and bedroll on the bare tick mattress, then took off his hat and hung it on a nail above the head of his bed. He looked around the room to get a fuller view of it.

There were a dozen bunks in all, two rows of six each, and only the first three in each row were in current use. Along the back wall, the cot closest to the table belonged to the young man named Brad. Then came Aden's, followed by the bunk that now held the belongings of the departed puncher. Along this wall, Will's was the farthest from the door, then Jim's, and then a bed that had all the signs of occupancy and must be the foreman's.

On the other side of the entry area where he had come in, a cast-iron stove sat quiet and dusty. To the left of it, in the corner, a small stack of firewood lay next to a heap of shavings. In the other corner stood a broom and an ax. A few feet from the corner, behind the table where Jim was sitting again, a door gave access to the area in back, where Will imagined he would find the outhouse, the woodpile, and the rubbish heap. An unlit lantern hung from a nail next to the doorway.

Will recalled the foreman saying that the next building over was the cookshack. That went along with what he saw here in the bunkhouse—no cookstove or eating area. He wondered what sort of a person ran the cookshack. Probably a quarrelsome old man who lived in his boar's nest and ran his domain like a tyrant.

No hurry for that, Will thought. In the meanwhile he'd get settled into his place and try to get a night's sleep. He didn't like being just across the aisle and one bunk over from Aden, but he figured Ingram's authority accounted for something.

Will set his bag beneath the bunk and rolled out his bed. Then he pulled off his boots and stretched out on the bunk. One step at a time, he told himself. As he got the lay of the land and a sense of which men he could trust, he could ask about Al Vetch. Remembering his original purpose, he amused himself by imagining what Mrs. Welles might be doing. He pictured her sitting by a lamp and reading newspapers to see if her husband had made the news by getting himself arrested or killed.

As Will dozed off, he had a dream in which the pleasant Mrs. Welles, smiling, approached him and offered him a derringer. Then he awoke at the sound of a chair scraping against the wood floor.

Jim was standing up and stretching. The foreman must have gone out back, as he was not around. The young dark-haired fellow named Brad had tucked himself into his bedroll, while Aden sat on the edge of his own bunk, pulling a sock between his big toe and the next one.

"About time to turn in," said Jim. "We'll hit it tomorrow. Do you need anything?"

"I don't think so." Will reviewed the question and his answer. He could think of things he'd like to have, but as far as needing anything, not a single image came to mind.

The cookshack was a bright place to walk into from the dark of early morning. Two lanterns hung above the mess table, and more light poured out of the kitchen area. Aden, wearing a plain drab work shirt and his denim jacket, sat at the table smoking a cigarette. His hat brim shaded his eyes, and as Will took a seat across the table and down a ways, Aden turned his head aside in an apparent snub.

Will poured himself a cup of coffee from the pot sitting on the table. He could hear clattering from the kitchen, and the smell of fried food—bacon, he thought—came drifting on the air.

Ingram took a place at the table, followed by Jim and then Brad. The young man sat on the other side, near Aden, who was the only one wearing a hat. The foreman poured coffee for the other two who came in behind him.

A form appeared in the kitchen doorway, and Will looked up to see a woman in a light-colored smock carrying two platters of food. One had a stack of bacon, and the other had a heap of fried potatoes. As she set the platters on the table, Will got a look at her.

She had a flushed, swollen complexion that might have come from hovering over a steaming kettle or from furtive nips on a bottle. Set into her face was a pair of pale blue eyes, and between them a thin nose protruded. Wrinkles were starting to show around her mouth, which she held in a pursed position, and below that her face ended in a soft chin. Her hair fell back across her ears on each side—straight, thin hair the color of last year's grass when a fellow turned over a plank. The skin below her jawline and on her throat had begun to sag, but overall she had the hardened look of a woman who had known how to attract men and how to brush them off. Will guessed her age at about thirty-five, and he imagined her dugs had begun to wrinkle. Then, catching again the pursed form of her mouth, he wondered if she had used her fair share of alum.

"Thanks, Blanche," said the foreman.

The woman made a sound like "Yuh" and went back to the kitchen.

During this whole fleeting moment, Will was conscious of hearing continued sounds in the kitchen. He figured there must be a second person working there. From time to time over the next several minutes as he ate his breakfast, he glanced at the doorway. He saw

Blanche's form move back and forth, but he could not catch a glimpse of the second person.

When the food had disappeared and the men were drinking their second cup of coffee, Ingram took out a silver watch and wound it. As he put it away, he began to speak.

"Dryden, we ride out in pairs. You'll go with Calvert—that's Jim—and he'll tell you the routine. I think you know the general rules, and for God's sake don't swing a loop at any animal that's got someone else's brand on it. You want to haze it away, fine, or slap it on the ass, but don't rope it."

"Sure."

Ingram brought out a toothpick now. "There's a couple of other outfits that are jealous, and they've got nothin' better to do than put a man out on a high spot with a pair of high-powered binoculars."

Will nodded.

The foreman looked across the table at the other two riders. "Max, you and Brad go out as always." Ingram took a last sip of coffee. "Well, I've got things to look into. I'll see you all back here at dinner."

Will got up from the table, and Jim Calvert did the same. They put their eating utensils in the wreck pan and went outside, where the sky was showing gray.

Both men put on their hats. Calvert's was a dark, battered thing with a round crown and flattened brim. It looked natural on him.

"I'll show you where we get our horses," he said. "When we're just ridin' out like this, we usually use one in the morning and one in the afternoon. If we need to stay out all day, of course, we do that."

Will got his rope from his saddle and went with Calvert to the horse corral. He had noticed it the evening before, a good-sized corral with about ten horses that ate hay out of a rack. It looked as if each evening the men brought in the horses for the next day. With the exception of finding Aden at this ranch, Will had a favorable impression of the way it was managed.

Calvert pointed out a bay for Will to rope, then went after his own. A few minutes later, as they led their horses to the barn, Aden and Brad came out with ropes for their mounts.

The sun was coming up as Will and his riding partner jogged side by side out of the ranch yard.

"Here's the deal," said Calvert. "We ride out a couple of miles, split up, and each make a circle, or the better part of one. We're partway back here when we meet. Then we split up again, circle around, and so forth. I 'magine you know the pattern."

"I've done it a few times."

The other man smiled. "I thought so."

"Anything in particular we're keepin' an eye out for?"

Calvert waved his free hand. "The regular stuff—anything lame or sick, anything suspicious, like little out-of-the-way brandin' fires, or the smell of new-burnt hair. When we get out on the far end, we push our cattle back this way. Push any others farther out if you've got the time and it's not too much trouble. Make a general note of what's runnin' with what. You'll see about four or five brands, over and over."

"How about anything unbranded?"

Calvert sniffed. "See what it's runnin' with, and what brand, especially any mama cow, and remember where you saw it, if you can."

"All right."

They rode on for a couple of minutes until Calvert spoke again. "Any questions?"

Will cleared his throat. "Actually, I've got one. What happened to the last fellow?"

"Ben Forrester?"

"I guess that's him. The fellow whose stuff you moved."

"Oh, that subject's a little touchy. No one seems to know, and the bosses don't seem to want to talk about it. I don't think Earl likes having one of his men shot, but until someone knows more, there's not much to do."

"Where did it happen?"

"Not a mile from the ranch."

"No one else around?"

Calvert raised his eyebrows. "Well, the party that pulled the trigger, I suppose."

"In full daylight."

"Yessir. It was like this. Earl Ingram, Ben, and I were all working together, building a holding pen, about two miles north of the ranch, a little more. We run out of nails, so Earl sent Ben back to the place to get some more. He never made it."

"How about all the others? Where were they?"

The other man shrugged. "We'd just finished roundup, so the extra hands were gone. There were just the ones that are here now. So that leaves Max Aden and Brad Way. They were together, out south a few miles."

"Huh."

"I know what a man might think, what with Max bein' so disagreeable and all, but he was with Brad. And besides, he didn't have anything against Ben. No one did. Ben was an easygoin', likable young fella. Why anyone would want to do him in is a mystery."

"So it had to be someone from the outside."

"Yep. The big boss wasn't even on the ranch. He was off in Laramie City. You couldn't even suspect Blanche. She was with the other girl in the kitchen."

The other girl. Will reflected that he had not yet seen her or the big boss. "You think someone could have gotten him by mistake?"

"It could have been that, if someone was lookin' for a man who wore a hat like his."

The two men rode on for a few minutes without talking until Jim Calvert spoke again. "So you and Max crossed paths earlier in the day yesterday."

"We sure did. I don't know if he was liquored up or if he's like that all the time, but he was spoilin' for a fight."

"Oh, that's just Max. Accordin' to him, he won a couple of bare-knuckle fights back in Missouri, for prize money. Now he thinks he's got to try to knock off anyone new that comes along. He rode the hell out of a couple of fellas that were here on roundup."

"The rest of you seem to take him all right."

Calvert waved his free hand again. "Aw, with me and Earl it's like water off a duck's back, and Max knows it. As for Brad Way, he's just naturally the kind that lets others have their way. Like with horses—one does the bitin' and kickin', and the other takes it. All the way down the line. Get six horses in a bunch, and one'll end up at the bottom of the order. That would be Brad." Calvert shrugged. "I guess that's why Earl has 'em work together. No friction."

"Makes sense."

"Me, I get along, too, but I ain't nobody's whippin' boy."

"Good way to be. I wish I was better at it. I let Aden get under my skin. He just wouldn't let up."

"Well, I guess he found out how far he could go with you, and you heard what Earl said about fighting. So I wouldn't worry until I had a reason to."

Which might be too late, Will thought. But he said, "I suppose."

Full daylight had spread over the plains when Will and Jim Calvert split up. Will felt the sun on his back and the cool morning air on his face as he put his horse into a lope. He felt the freedom of being back in the saddle on the open range, riding alone and ready to see what was over the next rise.

About an hour and a half later, the two men met as planned. They dismounted and sat in the shade of their horses. Calvert brought out his pipe and a tobacco pouch, and Will went about rolling a cigarette.

"Gittin' the lay of the land?" asked the other man as he stuffed his pipe.

"Somewhat. Pretty dry country. I didn't see any water at all where I went."

"There's water holes, a couple of 'em made with a scraper, but they're few and far between." Calvert struck a match, laid it across the bowl of his pipe, and started puffing.

Will rolled his cigarette tight and licked it. "No windmills?"

"Most of them are close to the ranches, and I'd guess all of 'em are on deeded property."

"This is all open rangeland out here, then."

Calvert handed him the match, still lit. "That's right. By the way, did you see any sheep? I forgot to mention them earlier."

"Didn't see any at all. I did see some wild horses, though, way the hell and gone." Will lit his cigarette and stuck the match in the dirt.

"Oh, yeah. They're out here. They keep their distance, of course."

The men smoked in silence for a couple of minutes until Will spoke. "This horse I'm ridin', I assume it's one out of Ben's string."

"That's right. You took his place. His string, his ridin' partner." Calvert smiled as he blew out some smoke. "Take what you git."

"Oh, that's all fine. I was just wonderin', though, what kind of horse he was ridin' that day."

"It was a sorrel out of his string, the one with a narrow blaze and two white socks. You'll get to ride him."

"Did he have a horse of his own?"

"Yes, he did. Nice little buckskin. It's out in the horse pasture still. When Earl figures out what to do with his other belongings, he'll probably do something with the horse as well."

"Did he get buried here?"

"Ben? Oh, yeah. We buried him in town."

Will nodded. Cowpunchers saw enough of death, most often mishaps out on the range, that they didn't talk about it very much. Some of them couldn't stand to hear the song "Bury Me Not on the Lone Prairie"; he figured it was because the cowboy in the song got buried there after all.

Calvert tamped his pipe with an empty rifle casing and puffed again. Then he set his old hat back on his head and in a cheery tone said, "How'd you like our hash slinger?"

"Blanche?"

"Uh-huh. I thought I saw you gettin' a look at her."

Will raised his eyebrows. "I imagine she's a fine figure of a woman, in some men's eyes."

Calvert laughed. "I suppose. But I haven't seen anyone on our crew motherin' up to her."

"I don't think I'll be the first."

Will and his new partner rode two more circles, and when they met on the last one, the sun was straight up.

"Time for the dinner bell," said Calvert. "Let's see what the cook has for us."

"Sounds good," said Will. As they put their horses into a trot, he wondered if he'd get to see the other girl in the kitchen, as Calvert had called her.

Chapter Four

In the full light of midday, Will could see the red-veined tinted hue of the sandstone that the ranch house and its smaller appurtenant building were made of. He had noticed the stone the evening before but had not seen the color, so now the name of the ranch made more sense.

Will and Calvert watered their horses and led them into the barn, where the men unsaddled and brushed the animals. Both horses had worked up a light sweat. After checking his mount for nicks and sores, Will took him out to the corral, where Jim Calvert had already left his horse and was waiting with the gate. Will led the bay in, made him turn around, and slipped off the halter. The horse went to the hayrack to join the one Calvert had just turned loose.

Before he left the corral, Will walked to the south end and looked across the top rail where the horse pasture stretched away. Will rolled and lit a cigarette. He figured the area for a quarter section, fenced in square about a half mile each way. Some twenty-five horses were scattered across the pasture, grazing. Will picked out his own horse, which was dark brown with a long, thick tail. Beyond it he saw the only buckskin in the pasture, a medium-sized horse that grazed with a couple of sorrels.

Will turned and walked to the gate, where Calvert stood waiting.

"Everything in order?" asked the other man.

"Looks like it."

"Let's clean up, then."

Will stood at the end of the horse trough and worked the pump handle while Calvert, having set his hat on a post, washed his hands and face. Will took a last drag on his cigarette and stepped on the butt. Then he set his hat where Calvert's had been and washed the morning's dust from his face. He splashed himself a couple of extra times, cupping the water with both hands and leaning his face down.

"Feels good," he said.

"Next best thing to a mountain stream."

Calvert led the way to the cookshack, where the two of them went in and sat at the table, each setting his hat on the bench next to him. No one else had arrived yet, and no food had been set out. The usual noises came from the kitchen—a clatter of plates, the thumping of a spoon on the lip of a pot, the creak of oven hinges. The current that wafted from the kitchen carried the aroma of boiled beans.

After a few minutes, Earl Ingram came in and sat next to Will. "How did it go?" he asked as he took off his hat.

"Just fine. Got to know a few brands."

"Nothing peculiar?"

Will shook his head. "All normal."

Aden and Brad Way came in, hung their hats, and sat across the table from Will and the foreman. Brad sat in the middle with Calvert on one side and Aden on the other.

Earl cocked his eyebrows and said, "Well, what'd you see, boys?"

"Nothin'," said Aden in a muffled voice.

Brad shook his head.

"Now that I think of it," said Calvert, "I saw something. It was a bull I don't remember seein' before."

The foreman turned to him. "Not some of that old stock, I hope."

"No, he was polled. Looked like he might be half Durham."

"That's not so bad. Did you give him a push anyway?"

"Oh, yeah."

At that moment Blanche made an appearance, holding her head back in a squint as she carried a steaming pot. When she set it down, Will saw that it was a pot of beans.

Blanche retreated to the kitchen and came back with five crockery bowls, which she set down with a thump and a clatter. By the time the men had the bowls distributed, she had returned with two tin plates of biscuits. Then from the pocket of the apron tied around her waist she produced five spoons, which she dropped on the table where the bowls had been. By the time the spoons settled, she was gone.

All this time, Will kept an eye out for the other kitchen girl, but she was yet to be seen.

Each man spooned himself a bowl of beans and grabbed a biscuit. Will thought the beans were a little soupy, but as he stirred his bowl he saw chunks of bacon rind with remnants of fat attached. He knew it took a lot of boiling to soften the rind, just as it took some muscle to cut it up beforehand. When he saw beans cooked this way, he recalled the first time he worked for a cow outfit. He was the night wrangler and cook's helper, and the old chuck wagon cook, McGuire, always gave him the task of cutting up the bacon rind. The stuff was greasy to hold and tough as leather to cut. Will doubted that Blanche would do that drudgery if she had someone to order around. He wondered if it was a hefty woman who could bear down on the knife.

Will noticed that Aden and Brad Way salted their grub before they tasted it, while Calvert and Ingram ate theirs as it was. Will tried a spoonful and decided it had enough salt, so he settled into the meal.

His mind drifted from one little thought to another, and he had forgotten about the kitchen help, when a dark-haired girl appeared with a pot of coffee.

His pulse jumped, and he looked up to get a view of her. Her dark hair was tied back with a cloth around it and fell loose from there, so that her full face was visible. She had a clear brown complexion, dark eyes, and a firm, serious mouth. She was of average height for a woman, and she had a fair to medium figure apparent beneath her loose work dress, which was made of a plain brown cotton cloth. Will guessed her to be in her early twenties—old enough to work away from home, wherever that was. He got another quick overall look. If she wasn't full Indian, she was at least half.

"Thanks, Pearl," said the foreman.

"Anything else?" she asked, showing her clean, even teeth.

Ingram glanced around. "I don't think so."

She hesitated, as if to make sure, and Jim Calvert spoke up.

"Pearl, this is our new man, Will Dryden. Thought you ought to know him in case he shows up bummin' a biscuit. Will, this is Pearl, the best of the best."

She blushed, giving a pretty glow to her bronze cheeks. "Nice to meet you," she said in a clear voice.

"A pleasure to meet you." Will smiled. He tried to think of something else to say, but he felt clumsy.

"Anything else?" she asked again.

"No, thanks," said the foreman. "Everything's fine."

The girl turned and went back to the kitchen, leaving Will with the sense that Ingram had dismissed her. Will reminded himself that he was just the hired man, and he didn't think the foreman had a personal interest in the girl anyway.

No one spoke for the next few minutes. Spoons clacked against crockery, the biscuits nearest to Will disappeared, and the sounds of eating were audible. Calvert reached for the coffee cups, which sat upside down in a group at the end of the table, and he passed them around. He poured himself a cup of coffee and handed the pot to Brad Way. The coffee went around the table, and one by one the men served themselves a second helping of beans. Blanche appeared with two more plates of biscuits, and Ingram thanked her.

At the end of the meal, everyone but Ingram had a smoke—Calvert with his pipe, and the other three rolling their cigarettes.

"Good grub," said the foreman.

"That's right," Calvert answered. "Nothing like the real thing. I remember I worked for a fella, just me and him and another puncher. We'd work sun to sun every day, go out on long rides with no grub. Then he'd serve us up a dab of somethin' for supper and say, 'Gittin' down to the bottom here, but we'll eat good tomorrow.' He said that just about every day."

Ingram took the toothpick from his mouth. "Penny wise and pound foolish. Fortunately, some outfits know better."

While Will recognized the comment as typical praise for the company, it also reminded him that he was yet to see or meet the big boss.

After noon dinner, Will and Calvert saddled fresh mounts and rode out to the southwest for an afternoon of the same routine. When they had ridden a good quarter mile out, Calvert spoke.

"Well, you got to see the other half of the kitchen help."

"The better half, at least by some standards."

Calvert laughed. "She's all right."

"Is she Indian?"

"Uh-huh. Sioux, I think."

"I wonder how she got a name like Pearl."

Calvert shrugged. "Common enough name. Men have it as well as women. I heard it was a favorite with Queen Victoria."

"The name?"

"No, the pearl itself, and the color."

"Huh."

"She says her father went over there with Buffalo Bill's show and met the Queen. I believe it."

"Fancy that."

"I guess the Indians liked the Queen. Buffalo Bill did a special show for her, and afterwards she met some of them. They call her Grandmother England, from what Pearl told me."

"How'd she end up here?"

"She doesn't want to be a blanket Indian, I suppose."

"Well, that's good." After a few seconds, Will added, "Does Blanche keep her under lock and key?"

"Blanche keeps the lard under lock and key. Or at least under her heavy hand."

"Can't complain about the grub, though."

"Oh, no."

Will thought for a second. "Those two women don't go out with the wagon, do they?"

"Not at all."

"Who cooks out on the range?"

"I do, whether we're out on roundup or whether we go out there for a few days somewhere." Calvert turned and gave an amused look. "No one complains then, either."

Will smiled. "After the story you told, I'm not afraid."

"No reason to be. Even if I do say so myself, when I cook, we eat good."

Will reflected again. "Does the boss go out with the wagon?"

"The old man? He drops in, maybe sleeps one night in the bed wagon. He's not one to sleep out on the ground or drink his coffee from a can."

"Is he gone right now?"

"No, I think he's around. You'll probably see him at supper."

A little farther on, the two riders split up, and Will was left to his own thoughts. Riding the range was a natural activity for him, but he wondered if he fell into it too easily, as if by doing something he knew how to do he was letting himself get sidetracked. As he sorted things out, he reinforced the idea that as long as he was here at the Redstone, anything he learned might help him find the missing Al Vetch. And there were things to learn. First off, there was the death of Ben Forrester. The young man got killed for something, and no one seemed anxious to find out why or even to dispose of his personal property.

A lesser question to ponder was the huffy behavior of Blanche the cook. Will did not expect her to be gracious to a crew of working men, but he didn't think she should be so brusque, either. The thought occurred to him that she might spend some of her time in private service to Donovan, in which case she might consider herself superior to men of her own class. Will figured he would form a clearer idea of that possibility when he saw the boss in the cook-shack.

Out on the far end of his ride, Will came across something that caught his interest. In the midst of broad, broken country with deep gashes and large upthrusts, he found where the side of a ridge had been laid open and heaps of rubble lay scattered at the base. Riding closer, he recognized the red-veined tint of the sandstone he had seen back at the ranch. This must be the quarry. Still thinking that he might find Al Vetch facedown in some desolate spot, he rode his horse through the ruins. Aside from tin cans, bottles, and a few odds and ends of rusted broken cable, he saw nothing but discarded rock.

When he met up with Calvert an hour later and the two of them dismounted for a smoke, Will told him of the place he had found.

"That's the quarry, all right. No one's used it for years. Good place for snakes, accordin' to Earl."

"It must have been a lot of work to cut all that stone and haul it back to the ranch."

"I'm sure it was," said Calvert, stuffing his pipe. "That was back when someone had the time and money for that sort of thing."

"Not in Donovan's time, then."

"Nah. He's only been here ten, eleven years. No one has worked that rock pile for over twenty years, I'd say."

Will shook his head. "Lotta work."

"I'd say. I'm glad I missed it."

Will licked his cigarette and tapped the seam. "Always amazes me. No matter how hard the work is, there's always someone who'll do it. Layin' track, buildin' trestles and stone bridges. Puttin' up tall buildings in cities. Haulin' bricks and mixin' mortar ten stories in the air, mountin' big blocks of stone on county courthouses. Some people must be born and bred to work like ants."

"Not me," said Calvert, passing the match. "This line of work is rough enough, but at least you're on your own a good part of the time. You can feel the breeze in your face, and when you want to stop for a smoke, you don't have an Irishman crew boss on your ass."

"Did you ever work on the railroad?"

"No, but I worked on a ditch crew, breathin' dust down where there wasn't a breath of air." Calvert puffed out a cloud of smoke. "The one thing that was interesting was what the dirt looked like down there."

"Layers and such."

"That's right. Gives you an idea of your future home. But even that doesn't hold your interest for long."

"I guess not. How long did you work there?"

"Two days. Then I went to punchin' cows, and I've been doin' that ever since."

Will took a long drag on his cigarette and blew out the smoke. "Sometimes I wonder what I'll do when I can't do this anymore."

Calvert wrinkled his nose. "I try not to think about that."

"Oh."

"If you think about it too much, you realize you might not get the chance to do somethin' else."

Will sat on the edge of his bunk as he and the other men waited for the supper bell. Calvert said it was the one meal of the day when Blanche beat the triangle, and Will could see that the men had their routine of killing time until the call came.

Aden, seated at the table with a cigarette in his mouth, was digging at his left hand with his jackknife. "Damn sandburs," he said to Brad Way. "Takes months to get 'em out."

Brad gave a nod of agreement, then went back to scraping the tar off a pair of elk ivories.

Ingram, who sat in a relaxed pose next to the table, said, "It's a wonder you get sandburs in your hands when you always wear gloves."

"I told you at the time," said Aden petulantly, "it was durin' fall roundup, and we were brandin' a few calves that slipped past us earlier. I had my knife out to cut this one big bull calf, so I wasn't wearing gloves. That son of a bitch had sandburs all up and down the hair on his back legs, and when he started kickin', I grabbed a leg and got a handful of burs jammed square into me."

"Did you get him cut all right?" asked Calvert, who was smoking his pipe and sitting in a chair near the open door.

"You damn right I did. He bellered and bellered, but he was a steer when he got up."

"It's better to get 'em when they're small anyway," said Ingram.

"Of course it is," Aden snapped. "But we didn't have any choice on this one." He winced as he dug the point of his knife into the heel of his hand. Smoke was curling up in front of his face now, so he took a long drag on the cigarette and squashed the butt end in an empty sardine can.

Will observed something he had noticed at noontime—the yellow stains on Aden's right hand. The man no doubt took off his gloves to roll cigarettes and then smoke them, so his twenty or thirty cigarettes a day burned down to a stub between his thumb and first two fingers. All that tobacco probably helped him stay wound up tight.

"Do you need a magnifying glass?" asked Calvert. "I've got one, and some needles, too."

Aden stuck his knife in the tabletop and pinched at the heel of his left hand. "Nah. What I need is for these sons of bitches to work their way out. They build a callus around 'em, and you dig out the dead skin, and the sticker's still down in there. They got a little hook on 'em. All you end up with is pocked-up hands."

"Take warnin', Brad," said Calvert, pointing his pipe at him. "You get your hands too rough, and the girls won't let you play titty."

Brad smiled. "I'll be real careful."

At that moment the clear ring of the triangle carried in the ranch yard.

"That's us, boys," said Ingram as he stood up.

No one needed to be told. The men had all risen at once at the sound of the bell, and now they filed out. Calvert waited to go last.

After the men had taken their places at the table but before any food arrived, another man came in through the door. Will took him to be the boss, Donovan. He was an older man, maybe sixty or a little more, with a full head of gray hair combed to one side. He had a slight forward hunch to his shoulders, which were not broad to begin with. He wore a gray suit of lightweight cloth, a clean white shirt, and a brown gun belt with a white-handled pistol. The gun looked out of place on a man of his build and posture, for he was soft-bellied, and his belt hugged the underside of the white shirt.

"Here's Frank," said Calvert.

The boss took the seat nearest to the kitchen, gave a nod and a smile to the other men, and said, "I thought the weather was going to cool off a little, but it doesn't seem to want to."

No one answered. Will, sitting across the table and over one seat, observed the man's face as the smile faded. Donovan was clean shaven, with sagging cheeks and a wattled, wrinkled neck. Will couldn't resist the impression that the pale face resembled a plucked Christmas goose, even unto the fleshy nose, which with its large pores looked like the goose's tailpiece where the feathers had been pulled out.

Donovan reached into his coat pocket and brought out a pair of thick spectacles and a folded piece of paper. He put on the glasses, which magnified his blue eyes, and unfolded the paper. With his head raised and his lips pressed together, he scanned the sheet and then set it on the table between him and Ingram, who sat at his right.

"Here," he said, pointing with his index finger. "Do you recognize this parcel?"

"What's this, a land auction?"

"Correct."

Ingram frowned at the printed sheet. "No, I don't recognize it from the description. Wouldn't know if it's any good."

Donovan resumed his close-mouthed impression,

then took off his spectacles and put them in his pocket along with the refolded paper.

Ingram glanced at Will, and when the boss had smoothed out his jacket, the foreman said, "Frank, this is our new man, Will Dryden. A good all-around hand."

Will rose halfway and held out his hand, and Donovan did the same. Will felt the soft hand give under his grasp, and then the two men drew apart and sat down.

Donovan smiled blandly. "I always say, a ranch is no better than the men that work for it. And I learned a long time ago that the best way for me, at least, is to let a foreman take care of the operations. Able men like yourself don't need me to tell 'em how to do their job."

Will hesitated, not sure what to say after these two separate bits of praise from men who hardly knew him.

Calvert, who was passing out plates and forks, spoke up. "He's a good 'un. He rode two different horses today, and I didn't see him fall off once."

"They were both dog gentle," said Will. "Give me another chance tomorrow."

Donovan let out a little laugh. "Sounds like you're goin' to fit in just fine."

The talk came to an end as Blanche came in with a rush, hefting a platter of fried beefsteak in each hand. From the way she set the meat down and was gone as quickly as she had come, Will did not detect any notice between her and the boss.

Donovan, like the other men, had taken out his own knife and opened it. As Ingram served him a steak, he looked down at it as if he was wondering whether to buy it. His lips were pressed together as before, and beneath his sagging face there lurked an underlying hardness. Will thought the expression made quite a contrast with the easy smile and simpering comments of a moment earlier.

Blanche came back with the pot of leftover beans, then made a quick return with two tin plates of fresh biscuits. Again the boss paid no attention, while Blanche remained aloof as always, as if she were feeding prisoners of war.

Supper got under way, and for a few minutes no one spoke. Then the foreman, resting his knife and fork, said, "Good grub."

"It sure is," said Donovan. "I wonder if we shouldn't have some coffee." With his voice raised a notch, he said, "Where's Pearl?"

The dark-haired girl appeared at the kitchen doorway, in a posture of waiting for the boss's order.

"How about some coffee, girl?"

She disappeared and a few seconds later emerged with the coffeepot. She stood a couple of feet from Donovan's elbow, turned over a cup, and poured his coffee.

"Thanks, Pearl," he said with an upward glance and smile. Then as she stood there, as if waiting to be dismissed, the boss turned to Will. "When I said earlier that a ranch was no better than the men who worked there, I meant the women, too. You can't go wrong if you leave the kitchen in the hands of a woman or two. Not that men aren't good cooks, of course. We're just lucky here at the Redstone." He turned again to Pearl, who stood with a wincing smile. "That's fine," he said.

She set down the coffeepot and turned away. Donovan's gray head turned, and he watched her until she disappeared into the kitchen; then with the rigid cast to his face, he returned to his meal.

Earl Ingram broke the silence as he spoke to Will. "You'll see the truth of what Frank said about men being good cooks."

"Oh?"

"Yep. We'll be goin' out for a couple of days, and when we're out on the range, Jim's the cook."

"And a good one," chimed in the boss.

Aden spoke without looking up. "When will that be?"

Ingram paused with a piece of steak on the tip of his fork. "Either tomorrow or the next day, dependin' on what Frank wants."

Will looked at the boss, who was chewing with his chin tucked down. Either Donovan didn't really let the foreman run things, or Ingram liked to defer to the boss when he was around. As for Donovan himself, he seemed to have let his thoughts wander somewhere else—maybe to the kitchen girl, Will thought, or to the land auction, or to places a hired man would never guess at.

Chapter Five

Will took his place with the other riders as Ingram led the little party out of the ranch yard the next morning. The foreman had given the orders as he wound his watch after breakfast, so Will helped Calvert pack a camp outfit of provisions and utensils. Each man tied a bedroll onto the back of his saddle, and then Brad Way held the packhorse while Will and Calvert tied on the packs. The sun had cleared the hills in the east and was casting long shadows as the group moved out onto the trail.

Ingram had his usual air of command and self-assurance as he rode along with a toothpick in his mouth. He wore his brown wool vest as usual, plus a pair of snug-fitting brown leather gloves. In addition, now that he was out and away from the buildings, he wore a dark gun belt with a dark-handled Colt .45 in view. Will had noticed that Ingram tended to give orders on short notice, which was a common method of maintaining authority; now, as the foreman sat with his head raised in an almost-jaunty pose, he gave the impression that he was pleased with himself.

Off to the foreman's left and half a length back, the sullen Max Aden seemed to be wrapped up in his own form of self-satisfaction. He was decked out in his usual large-brimmed hat, denim jacket, large neckerchief, and prominent six-gun. His broad leather chaps went along with the *tapaderos* on his stirrups to suggest that he was accustomed to working in southern brush country. Then, as a finishing touch to his outfit, Aden wore a pair of buckskin gloves, tanned almost white, with long narrow gauntlet cuffs trimmed in short fringe and decorated with red and blue glass beads. As Will saw the gloves for the first time, he could imagine why Ingram had found them worth mentioning.

Next in line behind Ingram and Aden, Will rode next to Brad Way. Behind them, Jim Calvert led the packhorse. Each man had only one saddle horse for this excursion, which meant there wouldn't be much hard riding. As Ingram had sketched out the plan, the men would make a broad sweep of the country where they had been riding out each day. By the foreman's estimate, there were about a dozen mama cows out there with unbranded calves—enough to make this job worthwhile. The men would gather what they could the first day, spend one night out, and bring in the whole bunch the next day.

Calvert split off from the other riders and headed west, where he would have a noonday camp waiting. The other four went south for a couple of miles until Ingram split them. He sent Aden and Way southwest, while he and Will went almost due west. They were all to meet up with Jim Calvert at Popper Spring.

Will knew Donovan's two brands quite well by now—the Rafter Six and the Lazy P-Bar—and he knew where Popper Spring was located, so when the time came to split up with Ingram, he rode off into the broken country without much worry.

As he had done on his earlier rides, he kept an eye

out for anything unusual, but the vast, quiet country seemed all in order. Cattle grazed in small bunches, and he saw no sign of anyone having herded cattle, driven horses, made an out-of-the-way dry camp, or anything of that nature. As the sun climbed in the sky, a haze and a drowse hung over the rangeland. He picked up a Rafter Six cow with a bull calf and pushed them along ahead of him, so the day slowed down even more.

Ingram and Calvert were sitting in the narrow shade of a box elder tree when Will brought the cow and calf into the meeting place at Popper Spring. He let his horse drink at the water hole, then led him away and picketed him as the wary cow came in. Will sat on the ground with the other two men.

"One pair, huh?" said the foreman. "I didn't find anything. We'll see what the other boys bring in."

"Here's grub," said Calvert. He lifted a white flour sack to uncover a tin plate of biscuits and another of sliced beef, a simple meal sitting on the dry grass.

As Will had helped Calvert pack the food, he knew it had been cooked earlier and would be cold and dry now. He also noticed that Calvert had not made a fire, so the coffeepot hadn't come out of the pack. Still, food was food, and in a lot of places a fellow would have to wait for suppertime to have anything at all.

"We already ate," said Calvert. "Dig in."

Will saw that the plate of biscuits sat on top of a small stack of plates, so he slipped one out from underneath and served himself.

When he finished eating, he rolled a cigarette and stretched out to lean on his elbow and enjoy his smoke. He had just gotten comfortable when Aden and Way came into view with two pair.

"One of each," said Ingram, craning his neck to read the brands.

The cattle broke into a trot for the last fifty yards as they rushed to the water hole. Aden and Way came in at a walk, let the horses drink, then turned away from the water and dismounted.

"Will, go ahead and hold their horses," said the foreman. Then, catching a dark look from Aden, he said, "Better yet, get on your own horse and make sure these cattle don't wander too far. After dinner, you and Jim can take these three pair to the place where we'll camp tonight."

"Where's that?"

"Jim knows."

Calvert, who had sat forward and was ready to uncover the food for the other two riders, said, "It's that holding pen we built a little while back."

"Oh."

"Makes it easy," said Ingram. "No one has to stay up and ride night herd on a few head of cattle." He turned to the other two men. "Don't bother to tie up your horses, boys. Just hold 'em while you eat. We're not gonna be here that long."

Will rose to his feet, took a long drag on his cigarette, and dropped the rest on the ground, where he smothered it with his heel. A foreman who smoked would have told him to finish his cigarette, but Ingram with his toothpick didn't seem to care much for someone else's little pleasure.

The distance from Popper Spring to the holding pen was about six miles, which meant somewhere between twelve and eighteen for Will, who had to ride back and forth to keep the three cow-calf pairs headed together.

He and Calvert had the bunch watered and penned up by late afternoon. Will saw that the pen had a good location, as it was a hundred yards from a trickly little stream. Calvert showed him where they would set the camp. Then they stripped the horses, watered them, picketed them out to graze, and sat in the shade of a lone cedar tree to have a smoke.

"Slow work," said Will.

Calvert set his worn hat back on his head. "Oh, yeah, but I guess we've got time for it."

"Does it seem to you that a dozen pair is quite a few to have missed during roundup?"

"You'd think so, but some of those fellas we had in here weren't all that good. Some of 'em got sore from ridin', some of 'em couldn't rope worth a damn, and one of 'em was so weak I thought he came off a six-month drunk. So as far as missin' a few head, I'm not that surprised."

Will blew away a stream of smoke as he gazed at the corral. "So this is the pen you were building when that young fellow Ben met his bad luck."

"That's right."

Will shook his head. "You know, I haven't heard a single word about him from any of the others."

"That's curious, isn't it? And there was nothin' wrong with that kid."

"Was he friends with anyone else?"

"Oh, like I said before, he got along with everyone. I was his ridin' partner, so you could say we were pals. As for the others, it was just the normal, everyday talk with them, as far as I could tell." Calvert took a puff. "Then there's Pearl. He seemed to be interested in her."

Will perked up. "Was he sweet on her?"

"Somethin' like that. I don't know how far he got,

because he always had to go around Blanche. I tried not to pay any attention, and I think the others did the same."

"How about Aden?"

Calvert wrinkled his nose. "I don't think Max cares about her. He doesn't like anyone who isn't white, and he doesn't even like most of them."

"That's just as well. And what about the boss?"

"The old man?"

"Yeah, him. Do you think he'd get jealous?"

"Well, on one hand, I don't think he's got that much lead in his pencil, especially with her bein' that much younger, but on the other hand, he does seem to favor her."

"I had that impression."

"Might be. Seems to me that he sees her more like a pet."

Will shrugged. "You'd think he'd be more likely to have an interest in Blanche, what with her bein' closer in age and type, but I haven't seen any spark at all there."

"No, I don't, either. Like I said, he doesn't seem to have much git-up-and-go, at least in that way."

Ingram, Aden, and Way came into camp with four more pair as the sun was going down behind the hills in the west. The first three pair had settled down somewhat, and now the commotion started again with cows lowing, calves bawling, and a continued milling of the restless animals. Grunts and whoofs came from the pen, and dust hung in the air.

Darkness had fallen by the time the horses had all been put out and the saddles and bedrolls had found their respective places around the camp. With the scraps left over from the poles and rails of the pen,

Calvert had gotten a good campfire. He had two twin plates heaped with bronzed salt pork and two more with potatoes fried in the pork grease. A blackened coffeepot sat on a rock at the edge of the fire where the coals were banked, while the other half of the fire blazed with fresh fuel and cast light out into the campsite.

The five men sat down to eat at the same time. Calvert divvied up the food on five plates, and each man sat with his plate balanced in his lap.

"Some of this seems like a lot of extra work," said Brad Way. "We've driven a couple of these pair nearly all day from the southwest, and then we'll drive 'em south to the ranch tomorrow."

"Sure," said Ingram. "We could brand 'em one by one out on the range, but all you need is for someone to challenge you on one calf, and you've got more quarrel than you need. We'll take 'em all back and brand 'em together in the big corral."

Aden's voice came up, unexpected. "It's the Texas way," he said. "Never brand outside a corral."

"We've got a corral right here," Brad answered.

Ingram's voice was firm. "We'll take 'em all back. It's what Frank wants."

"The Texas way," said Calvert. "I'm not from Texas, but I know for damn sure it wasn't always that way there. Hell, that's where the long rope started, and boys from there'll tell you how it was every man for himself. A fella slapped his brand on every unbranded calf he found, anywhere he found it. And that wasn't so long ago."

"Times are changin'," said Ingram.

"Oh, I know. One of the best changes in Wyoming was when they dropped the Maverick law. When it was goin', you couldn't brand your own stock outside a roundup supervised by the association. Thank God those days are gone."

"Well," Ingram said, "we're doin' it the way Frank wants. It's a good way and a safe one."

Back at the ranch, the crew had eleven calves to brand—four with the Rafter Six brand, and seven with the Lazy P-Bar. Ingram laid out the procedure after breakfast in the cookshack as the other men smoked.

"Will, you and Brad can run 'em into the alleyway. We'll do the Rafter Six calves first, then the Lazy P-Bar. Bring one pair at a time into the chute. Push the calf into the big corral, and turn the cow into the pen. As we go through 'em, they all go into that pen. So we just separate one calf at a time, and only for as long as it takes to brand 'im." He turned to Aden. "Max, you'll do the ropin', so saddle yourself a good horse for that."

"Two of us do the wrestlin', then?" asked Brad Way.

"That's right. However you want to do it. Meanwhile Jim runs the fire and makes sure I get the right iron each time." Ingram looked around. "All clear?"

The men nodded.

"Good enough. Let's get started and see if we can get done before it gets hot out there."

By the time Will and Brad had the cattle in the alleyway and the first pair in the chute, Aden was mounted and waiting in the corral. He had his denim jacket tied to the back of his saddle and held the coils of his rope in one gloved hand and his loop in the other.

He roped the first calf, a dark brown heifer, as it broke from the chute into a run. He had his rope tied hard and fast, Texas style, and as soon as he caught the calf he stopped the horse short. The calf kept running, and when it hit the end of the line a second later, the force jerked it to the ground. Aden's horse trotted forward to drag the calf to the fire. When the horse stopped, the calf scrambled to its feet.

"Flank him!" hollered Aden.

Will followed the rope down to the calf's neck, reached across the animal's back, grabbed a flank with one hand and a front leg with another, and flopped the kicking, writhing critter onto the ground. Will sat on the front shoulder and kept a hand on the rope while Brad Way pulled out the upper hind leg and held down the lower leg with his booted feet. Dust hung in the air as the calf struggled against the stretching.

Jim Calvert came at a fast walk from the fire. "Hot iron! Rafter Six, heifer calf."

He handed the iron to Earl Ingram, who stood at the calf's back and set his left foot on the animal's hip. Will smelled the burned hair as Ingram branded the calf on the flank—not so shallow that the brand could be changed easily, and not so deep as to injure the animal. Nevertheless, the heifer gave a burst of resistance, bawling as it tried to flail its legs.

Ingram stepped back and said, "Let 'er up." Then he handed the iron to Calvert, who returned to the fire.

Will loosened the rope around the calf's neck and slipped the loop off around the animal's nose. Before he had his fingers clear of the rope, the loop jerked away, twisting a finger and warming the tips of all four. He looked up to see Aden, nonchalant, reaching to catch the sailing loop. Will turned to nod at Brad Way, who was waiting for the signal. They let go of the calf, which thrashed its way onto its feet and ran bawling toward its mother. Will and Brad pushed the calf into the pen and then went for the next calf. Aden, who had coiled his rope and rebuilt his loop, sat on his horse waiting.

The second calf went pretty much the same as the first, falling with its back in the same direction, so Ingram did not have to change position. As before, the smell of burned hair mixed with the stirred-up dust, and a minute later the calf stood up with an inverted *V* over a number six seared into its hide.

The third one was the bull calf Will had rounded up the first day. Husky and thick-necked, this one gave resistance from the beginning. After Will flanked him he got back up, so Brad Way had to tail him down as Will yanked the rope.

Jim Calvert came at his fast walk. "Hot iron! Rafter Six, bull calf."

"Hold him still!" barked Ingram.

Brad pulled on the leg as Will strained on the rope. The smell of singed hair rose from the animal's side.

"That's got it." Ingram handed the iron to Calvert and reached into his pocket. "Let's cut him." He called over his shoulder, "Jim, you hold one leg while Brad holds the other."

Will kept his place on the front quarter, pulling on the rope. As the other two men pulled on the hind legs and held them apart, the foreman leaned down and castrated the calf. He slit the scrotum, pushed out a testicle, teased the cord with his knife blade, and then did the same to the second testicle.

Ingram straightened up and said, "Go ahead and

take the rope off." He clicked his knife closed as he stepped back.

Will took care to keep his fingers free, but Aden gave it a full effort anyway, jerking the rope so hard that the loop went whistling past the tip of Will's nose.

Jim Calvert gave the leg he had been holding to Brad Way. Then he stood up and stayed clear. The two wrestlers let the calf up, and as they herded it toward the pen where its mother stood lowing, Will saw Ingram toss the testicles in the fire.

"Let's get the next one," called the foreman. "Should be one more Rafter Six. Brindled cow and calf. Make sure they're together. Max, back up a little."

Aden, who had his coiled rope tucked beneath his arm and was flexing his hands in their neat-fitting gloves, tipped his head up without a word and reined his horse backward a few steps.

Brad Way spoke softly in Will's direction. "Look out for this next cow. She's a mean one."

At that moment, a movement beyond the corrals caught Will's eye, and he saw Blanche's pale form moving across the ranch yard.

Aden's voice came across the corral from behind Will's back. "Aw, don't be afraid of that old bitch."

Will laughed, and when Brad looked at him, he just shook his head. Brad stuck the pole in between the rails of the chute, nudging the brindled cow forward and then lodging the pole behind her haunches so she couldn't back up. In an even lower voice he muttered, "Easy for him to say."

"Yeah. I was laughing at something else." Will glanced across the top rail again to see if he could catch another glimpse of the cook, but she was no longer in sight.

That afternoon, with the calves branded and all eleven pair turned out to pasture, the men were to look after their horses and gear. With the help of Jim Calvert, Will got all seven horses in his string put into one corral. He led them one by one to a hitching rail in front of the barn, where he combed and brushed them and examined their legs and feet.

Aden took one of his horses out on a ride. Brad Way and Jim Calvert worked with their horses inside the barn, in the shade. Will did not mind working in the sun, as he caught what little breeze came through and he could observe any other movement in the ranch yard.

At about an hour after dinner, Earl Ingram went to the ranch house, knocked on the door, and was let inside. A little while later, Blanche's form crossed the space in back between the cookshack and the bunkhouse.

Will's heartbeat picked up. Now would be a good moment to talk to the kitchen girl, even if all he did was get himself on speaking terms with her.

Taking care not to hurry, he crossed the open yard and went in through the front door of the cookshack. He noticed that the back door was closed, and he thought that was in his favor.

"Anyone here?" he called out, hoping Blanche couldn't hear him from the outhouse.

A shuffling sound in the kitchen was followed by the appearance of Pearl in the doorway.

"Hello, there," he said, taking a couple of steps toward her so he wouldn't have to speak loud.

"Good afternoon." Her eyes passed over him as she stayed in the doorway.

His eyes met hers, and he smiled. "I was wondering if I could get a dab of bacon grease. One of my horses has a cut on the ankle, down by the hoof, and it's swelled up. The salt in the bacon grease will take the swelling down, and the grease itself will seal up the cut."

She stood still, not speaking.

"You probably know that," he said. As she still did not move, he took in a roving glance of her dark eyes and hair, her white apron and brown dress.

"Let me see." She put her hand on the doorway and turned.

From the side, he appreciated her figure. She had a high bosom and firm hips, and he could imagine Ben Forrester having admired the same features.

She lowered her hand from the doorjamb and disappeared into the kitchen. As Will waited for her to come into view, the back door opened. Blanche stopped in her tracks with the bright daylight as her background.

"What do you want?" Her voice came out raspy, and her face hardened as the narrow eyes settled on him.

Will shrugged. "I just came to see if I could get some bacon grease to rub on a cut. One of the horses in my string has a cut on his pastern."

Blanche moved forward and closed the door behind her. "There ought to be some," she said in the same voice as before.

"I don't need much more than a dab."

"Pearl!" she called out as she turned toward the kitchen.

The girl came out in a rush, carrying a tin plate

with a large gob of pale, streaky grease in the middle. Blanche's voice stopped her.

"He doesn't need that much. Just put a couple of spoonfuls in a tin can."

Pearl lowered her head and did not look at either Blanche or Will. She went back into the kitchen, and silence hung in the air as Blanche, with her lips pursed, stared at the empty space beyond Will. Pearl reappeared, holding out a tarnished tin can. Her eyes met Will's for a fleeting second as she handed it to him, and she smiled as he thanked her.

"And thank you," he said to Blanche as the girl faded into the kitchen again.

"Anytime," came the rough voice. Then as Will turned to leave, she said, "You don't need to bring the can back."

The next day, when Will and Calvert were back on the routine of checking cattle, Will told about his encounter with Blanche and the bacon grease.

"She seems awfully suspicious," he said, rolling his cigarette. "And I haven't done a damn thing."

"Oh, you don't have to with Blanche."

"But she's on her guard so much, it just seems curious."

"Oh, it might be." Calvert tamped his pipe with the empty rifle casing, lit the bowl, and handed the match to Will.

"Maybe it's because I'm new, but the way she acts goes along with some other things that don't seem normal." Calvert gave a light toss to his head, but Will felt they had enough shared confidence for him to go on. "I can't make the connection yet, but here you've got a puncher who's been killed, a cook who's jumpy as hell, another puncher who acts like he could blow up any minute, a foreman who acts like nothin' is goin' on, and a big boss who talks like it's all one big happy family."

"I can't disagree with any of that," said Calvert, "but I try not to go out of my way to look for things wrong with the outfit." His teeth clacked against the pipe stem. "You ride for an outfit, and you try to mind your own business. Of course, if you see something you think is wrong, maybe you don't keep lookin' the other way all the time."

"I guess that's what I mean."

Calvert's eyebrows went up. "Furthermore, a fella's got to be careful who he talks to."

"Well, I'm sure not gonna repeat anything you say, and I'm not gonna share my impressions with anyone else on this outfit, either."

"I figured that."

"And as far as why I'm so curious, I think anyone would be if he came in and took over where a man got killed and everyone's mum."

"Oh, yeah. Same goes for someone whose ridin' partner got killed for no apparent reason."

Will looked at the ash on his cigarette. "And as scowly as Aden is, you don't think he had anything to do with it."

"No, I don't. Not this thing with Ben, anyway." Calvert palmed the bowl of his pipe and drew a couple of puffs. "I'm like you. I can't make the connection."

"I've got the feelin' that some of these people are in cahoots, but I don't know where to start."

Calvert shook his head. "Neither do I."

"Well, let's suppose a person started at the top, then."

"The old man?"

Will squinted as he took a drag on his cigarette. He knew that some punchers called the big boss or owner of an outfit "the old man" regardless of his age, but even at that, whenever he heard Donovan referred to by that term, he thought it made the man seem more harmless than he might be. "Yeah, him," he said. "He talks so sweet about everything, you'd think he's got to be coverin' up for something."

"Oh, he might be."

"He seems like he's got other irons in the fire."

"I believe he does."

Will paused. "Do you know what he's up to, then, other than honestly branding his cattle for all the world to see?"

Calvert tamped his pipe again and gave it a draw. "The way I understand it, he's tryin' to buy up land and push out the little fellas—homesteaders and the like. The story is, he's got a partnership of foreign investors, Englishmen or Scotchmen, that want to run a big herd of cattle. This is supposed to be in addition to his own holdin's."

"Huh. I wonder how that could lead to a young fella gettin' killed."

"That's what I can't see, either."

Will took a last drag on his cigarette and pinched out the narrow stub. "You don't think he was some kind of detective, do you? Some fella who worked his way into the crew so he could get information for a party who was leery of getting swindled, and then the swindlers found out?"

Calvert shook his head. "I don't think so. The kid was open about everything. He talked about his past, his family in Iowa. He got letters from home. I suppose a fella could make all that up, but I don't think he did. He wasn't that deep. Besides, he wasn't new.

He worked here last year and came back again this spring."

"Well, I guess we'll have to hang on to that part. How about the other part, about the investor deal? Do you think it's on the up-and-up?"

"I don't know. After all, no one has seen these foreign investors. Leastwise, they haven't come around here. I wouldn't be surprised if Donovan was buying up land for some deeper reason, but I don't know what it would be."

"Are there any other partners, like from around here, who have figured into this?"

"Not that I know of."

Will hesitated and then took his chance. "Have you ever heard of a man called Al Vetch?"

Calvert frowned. "No, I haven't. Who's he?"

"I'm not sure myself. Just someone whose name I heard, and I thought I should be on the lookout for him."

Calvert shook his head. "Sure doesn't ring a bell."

"And as far as that goes, I've never heard the name, either, much less repeated it."

"Then it's damn sure I've never heard it." Then in a louder voice, Calvert said, "I think bacon grease is a good idea. I use it on cuts and sores like that, too."

Chapter Six

In the gray light before sunrise, Will tied the sorrel horse to the hitching rail in front of the barn. Although he had brushed the animal and looked him over the day before and had led him around the yard before turning him into the corral to eat hay overnight, he had not ridden this horse. The last time the horse had been ridden, Ben Forrester had been shot from the saddle.

Will took his time brushing the horse, then combing the mane and tail. He laid on the saddle blanket, smoothed it to make sure it had no wrinkles, and placed the pad on top of that. Next he swung the saddle up and let it settle onto the horse's back. Still taking care not to make any abrupt movements, he reached under the barrel of the horse and drew the front cinch toward him. He ran the latigo through the cinch ring one, two, three times and snugged it. The horse hadn't blown up against the cinch, so Will buckled the rear cinch with no trouble. Next he brought the headstall up to the sorrel's ears and slipped the bit into his mouth. With the bridle in place, Will brought the neck rope up over the horse's ears and down past the nose, then passed the reins through it. He coiled the rope and tied it to the right side of his saddle, checked to see that the left one was still in place, and turned the horse away from the hitching rail to walk him out a ways.

The door of the cookshack opened, and Max Aden came striding out, his large-brimmed hat bobbing. His chaps made a rumpling sound as his boot heels struck the hard ground. He hawked and spit, then lifted a half-smoked cigarette to his mouth. The tip glowed as he took a drag.

Will had been the first one to leave the breakfast table, as he had wanted to be able to take his time with the sorrel. He hadn't paid much attention to the others, but he had been aware of Calvert and Brad Way going out to fetch their mounts. Aden must have had something confidential to discuss with the foreman, and now he was in a rush to get ready.

Will led his horse to the barn door and watched as Calvert and Way finished saddling their horses and led them out. Aden came in with a speckled white horse on his rope. He tied the animal, slapped the blanket on without shaking it or brushing the horse, and then swung the saddle high and let it slam into place with the stirrups rattling and the buckles jingling. He pulled the cinches quick and hard, giving the horse a knee in the ribs in case he had taken in air. As Aden took off the rope and held his arm around the animal's neck, he slipped on the bridle. In less than two minutes he had his mount ready to go, and he pulled on his whitish gloves as he led the horse outside. Without a word he swung into the saddle and took off at a trot, with Brad Way just turning out his stirrup and pausing to gaze at his impetuous partner. Then Brad swung aboard and trotted to catch up.

Jim Calvert, meanwhile, stood with a quizzical smile on his face. "You don't seem to be in nearly the hurry," he said.

"I wanted to take my time with this horse. I didn't know if he was going to be skittish. It doesn't look like it. Why don't you go ahead and get on, and then I will."

Calvert put his foot in the stirrup and swung on up. Will did the same, and as he settled in and caught his right stirrup, he felt the sorrel move out at a smooth, steady pace. Calvert looked back, Will nodded, and they were off on their morning ride.

Their work took them to a part of the ranch Will had not yet seen, east and a little south of headquarters. He noticed the grass was dry and sparse, and he found the small bunches of cattle at broad distances from one another. Almost all the cattle had Donovan's two brands, and he saw no unbranded calves.

The landscape itself held little variety, consisting of wide, rolling country with small dry-wash gullies. He did not come across any surprise canyons or sudden gashes, and after two hours of riding he could not remember having seen a single tree. A thin carpet of grass, cactus, and sagebrush, none of it stirrup high, stretched away in all directions.

Will found a high spot where, with his back to the sun, he could ponder this land that seemed almost empty. With its monotonous surface and its thin scattering of cattle, it offered little to study. As before, he had seen no evidence of shady enterprise—not so much as a lopped ear or tipped horn—and no sign of animals passing through. The landscape did not lend itself to out-of-the-way trails or tucked-away hidey-holes, and he concluded it must be poor country for rustlers and horse thieves.

As he squatted in the shade of the sorrel horse

and continued to gaze across the broad surface, he considered the obvious. If he saw nothing out of order with the livestock, then maybe everything was on the square in that area. Still, he believed his deep-down feeling that something was not right and that if he could put things together here at the Redstone, it would help him find Al Vetch. He gazed at the land again, as if he could read the answer, but all he got in return was a mute stare.

Will returned to another set of details that evening at supper. Donovan came to the cookshack, smiling as before and bobbing his head as he greeted each one of the hired men. Will noted again the sloping shoulders, the belly that sagged like a soft-boiled egg, and the gun belt that seemed out of place.

"This hot weather doesn't seem to want to let up," said the boss as he took his place on the bench.

"These boys like it," said Ingram. "They don't like to have things too easy."

Donovan gave a little laugh, put his hand on the white pistol grip, and shifted in his seat.

Ingram went on. "Take Max here. He wears a jacket up to the hottest part of the day. Then he's nice and cool when he takes it off."

Donovan turned his head and smiled, showing his wattled neck. "Is that right, Max?"

Aden kept his gaze on the table as he said, "It doesn't get hot here."

"It does to me," said Brad Way.

Donovan put on his smile again. "I think you and I are the same."

A movement from the kitchen caused Will to look up. Blanche came forward with two platters of beef fried in various sizes. She held back her florid face as she set the meat on the table, and she did not take any visible notice of the boss. He, meanwhile, sat with his nose wrinkled and his head raised, as if he was appraising his own generosity at the food being served.

A minute later, Blanche returned with two plates of fried potatoes. Again, she and Donovan seemed to ignore each other, but as she turned away, he spoke.

"Blanche, bring me a knife, would you? I don't have one."

She came back with a paring knife and laid it on the table next to his plate.

"Thanks," he said, without looking at her. "You could bring the coffee now, too."

Will waited as the other men served themselves. He was hoping Pearl would bring out the coffeepot, but Blanche herself delivered it, again without acknowledging that anyone sat at the table. Will caught another glance of Donovan, who was pushing down hard on the kitchen knife as he cut off a corner of meat. The older man's face had a rigid cast to it, with the corners of his mouth turned down. Then he lifted the small piece of meat, opened his mouth without changing the stiff expression, and began to chew with small, mincing movements.

Will served himself and cut into his piece of beef. It was tough, all right, probably shoulder meat from the grain of it, but it tasted good after a long day of dust and tepid water.

Ingram poured a cup of coffee for the boss and then one for himself. "Even though we don't like things to be too easy, everyone likes this part of the day."

"It's a welcome pleasure," agreed the boss. "Eat

good, sleep good, and feel good, whenever you can." He paused with his fork above his plate as he gave his bland smile. "That's what I've found. Keep your men well fed, and pay 'em an honest wage. Of course, some men aren't even happy with that, but that's all right, too. I always say, if a man's not happy where he is, don't try to keep him from goin' someplace where he thinks he'll have it better."

"Sure," said Ingram. "I've seen it. You've got a fella that thinks he should have a better job than night wrangler, and that's all you've got for him, and he up and quits. Then you find out he spent the rest of the season gettin' calluses from handlin' a pitchfork and a shovel."

Donovan dabbed at his mouth with a handkerchief. "All work is good work."

"Oh, yeah," agreed the foreman. "Lots of good men have done every kind of work."

No one else spoke for the next several minutes, so the only sounds came from the meal in progress. All the fried pieces of meat disappeared, as did the slices of potato. As the men took out their smoking materials, Donovan pushed his plate away and swung his leg over the bench.

"Well, that's it for me," he said. "I wish you all a good evening." As everyone returned the courtesy, he stood up and bobbed his head around, smiling. Then, with a glance at the kitchen door, he left.

Ingram took out his watch and wound it. "Seems like the grass turned dry early this year," he said. "Not much rain, and now this heat."

Aden shook out his match and blew a double stream of smoke through his nostrils. "It doesn't get hot here," he said. "People just think it does."

Will did not have anything to add to the topic of the weather, so he listened to the sounds from the kitchen. He could tell there were two people working there. He thought it was too bad Pearl hadn't come out, as he had not seen her since he asked her for the bacon grease, but he figured Blanche was keeping her on a close tether. Then again, Donovan didn't call for her, either.

Calvert spoke up. "Maybe folks think it's hot because it is to them. They just haven't suffered as much as you have, Max."

Aden rubbed his yellowed thumb against his index finger. "It's not *hot*," he said.

A slight breeze drifted through the bunkhouse from the back door to the front. Jim Calvert sat near the front door, as he often did, and smoked his pipe. Aden sat at the table, close to the lantern light, digging at the old sandbur spines in his left hand. Earl Ingram sat near the dusty wood stove, not far from the table. Brad Way sat on the edge of his bunk, shaving the bark off a two-foot length of chokecherry wood about an inch and a half thick. Will lounged on his own bunk, the farthest from the center of the little gathering.

As the subject of the weather had pretty well run its course before the men left the supper table, the talk in the bunkhouse had been running to homesteaders and how a lot of them couldn't make it and had to sell out.

"Just as well," said Aden. "Go back where they came from. Half of 'em don't talk English. Swedes, Norwegians, bohunks."

Ingram seemed to ignore the comment. "Thing

is, it's hard to make a livin' on a quarter section. Especially when it's all grassland, and not very good grass at that. It's better if a bigger outfit can hold together a few sections, not have it cut up into so many little pieces. It can get some production then, even if it doesn't come to very much per acre. People want to raise crops, they should do it where there's more rainfall. Isn't that right, Jim?"

Calvert stuck his little finger in the bowl of his pipe. "A lot of people have gone broke tryin' to farm dry country, thinkin' the rain would follow the plow. It's a quaint notion, but faith doesn't water the crops."

Ingram went on. "This country was made for grazin', and it should stay that way. Look at what was here before—antelope and buffalo. Hell, the Indians knew better than to try to raise corn here."

"Anyone ought to," said Aden without looking up.

Brad Way spoke. "I think the ditch projects are changin' some of that. Like you said the other day, times are changin'."

"In some places," Ingram answered. "But there's no ditches here."

Brad paused in shaving the stick. "Up north and over east there are."

"Well, that's fine. They can water their alfalfa and corn, and have winter feed."

"More winter work on those places," Brad said. "Not that I'd care for some of it."

"Me neither," said the foreman. "Pitchin' hay in the ice and snow." He paused as a glow of recognition lit his features. "Say, Jim, that reminds me of something. That poem you recited last year. Do you still remember it?"

Calvert raised his eyebrows as he peered over

the bowl of his pipe. "I suppose I do. I made it up myself."

"You haven't forgotten it?"

"Oh, no. I run through it once in a while when I'm off on my own."

"Well, why don't you go through it now?"

Calvert looked around at the other men. "If no one minds."

Will nodded. "Sure."

"I'd like to hear it," said Brad. "I didn't know you made up poems."

"Didn't you hear it before?"

"Not if it was last year. You must be thinkin' of Ben."

"Go ahead," said Ingram. "You don't mind, do you, Max?"

Aden answered, again without looking up from his self-surgery. "I could hear it again."

Calvert stood up and cleared his throat by way of a short cough. "Well, here it is. I call it 'Thorns on the Rose.' It's kind of a story poem. I started it about ten years ago, and it just kind of grew on me." Then, in a singsong tempo, he delivered the poem.

A flaxen-haired maiden from Sweden
   Stepped down from the train in Cheyenne.
She said, "I'm a wheat farmer's sweetheart.
   I've come here to marry my man.

"I love him though I've never met him,
   His photograph I've never seen—
But here I am now in this city,
   To be his sweet bride at sixteen.

"He's written me long, lovely letters
   About the big farm he has here—
One hundred and sixty acres,
   And six months' vacation each year.

"He tells me I'll find it delightful
   Where winters are generally warm—
So please, if you can, won't you tell me
   The way to the Johnson farm?"

Well, the man she addressed was a cowboy
   Who'd just ridden in from the range.
He said, "If it's Johnsons you're seekin',
   There's a hundred from here to LaGrange.

"Them and their cousins, the Nelsons,
   They came out in droves from the East.
They're scattered all over the prairie,
   And plowin' it up to grow wheat.

"Not one out of ten has a woman,
   So lonesome it is on this land,
That long, lovely letters get written
   To make the adventure seem grand.

"You're young and you're sweet and you're
     pretty,
   And I hope you don't think I'm unkind,
But a maiden like you deserves warning,
   Before she walks into things blind.

"That six-month vacation you mentioned
   Will be spent in the ice and the snow,
Knockin' mud off the toes of the chickens,
   Milkin' cows when it's forty below.

"The other six months aren't much better
  With the wind and the dust and the heat,
Then a dark cloud that comes out of nowhere,
  With a hailstorm to flatten the wheat.

"On Monday you wash clothes for the baby,
  On Tuesdays you scrub and you bake,
On Wednesdays dig spuds in the garden
  And keep an eye out for the snake."

"Enough!" said the maiden, now blushing,
  "You're making me feel like a child.
Is there nothing out here in this country
  To make all the hardship worthwhile?

"If you weren't such a clear-eyed young
    fellow
  I'd think you were telling me this
To make me forget about Johnson
  And his promise of marital bliss.

"So tell me, young man, on your honor,
  What better things you can propose—
Is yours a soft life of warm sunshine
  Where harm never comes to the rose?"

"Oh, no," said the cowboy, still smiling,
  "The only rose I know is wild.
It blooms for a few days in springtime
  When the weather is fragile and mild.

"But the petals soon blemish and wither,
  And the rosebush goes back to the thorn.
So my life is not one to entice you
  And I fear it would make you forlorn.

"But there's one thing I have over Johnson,
   I can tell by the look in your eye—
You don't mind a straight-talkin' cowboy
   Who can't find it in him to lie.

"And at least you know what I look like—
   You don't seem repulsed by the clothes
Of an honest range-ridin' cowpuncher
   Who admits there are thorns on the rose."

"That's true," said the flaxen-haired maiden,
   "You seem to be honest and kind.
But a young girl has got to be careful
   With someone she meets the first time."

"It's all for the best," said the puncher,
   "To not take a step you'll regret,
And I hope you're convinced not to marry
   This wheat farmer you've never met.

"And if you don't mind, I'll invite you
   In the light of this warm afternoon,
To stroll through the cactus and sagebrush,
   And see the wild roses in bloom."

So off went the flaxen-haired maiden
   To stroll arm in arm with this man,
As meadowlarks sang to the whistle
   Of the train pulling out of Cheyenne.

If ever this story has a moral,
   It might go like this, I suppose:
Don't promise your love to a stranger,
   But don't fear the thorns on the rose.

Don't promise your love to a stranger,
But don't fear the thorns on the rose.

When Calvert finished the delivery, he gave a slight bow to the applause from the other men and sat down.

"That's quite a poem," said Ingram. "It's longer than I remembered."

"Oh, it's the same as it was last year."

"They do raise a lot of wheat there," Brad offered. "Dry-land farming."

"They do," said Calvert. "I was working for an outfit north of Cheyenne when I first started the song—or poem, I should say. The punchers were jokin' about all the wheat farmers named Johnson, and those first few stanzas kept runnin' through my head until I finally had to get 'em out."

Aden took an audible breath through his nose. "Cheyenne's a long ways from here. Even if they grow wheat there, that doesn't mean they can do it just anywhere."

Ingram took the toothpick from his mouth. "I like the part where he tells her what the work is really like."

"That's right," Brad Way agreed. "Of course he was doin' it for his own good, but he opened her eyes a little."

"Then he walks her down the primrose path," said Ingram. "Bright-eyed girl of sixteen, and him a worldly-wise cowpuncher. It sounds like you in the story, Max."

Aden still did not look up. "At least she's the right kind, even if she's a foreigner."

"You mean white," said Calvert.

"Blonde-haired."

"Maybe tomorrow I'll do a ballad about a dark-haired señorita or an Indian maiden."

Aden set down his knife and reached for the Bull Durham in front of him on the table. "I've heard a couple of them," he said. "One's about three old whores in Mexico, and one's about an Indian maid who puts sand up her flue."

Calvert rapped the bowl of his pipe on the heel of his boot. "You're always right in there with a smile and a good word, aren't you?"

Ingram spoke up. "What was the name of the outfit you worked for back then, Jim?"

"Fella named Herring. First name of Red."

"Red Herring? You must be kidding. Was that the real name?"

"Nah," said Calvert. "It was the Delmore outfit. But then the Swan Land and Cattle Company bought them out, and Tom Horn and a couple of others went to work for 'em, and it wasn't fun to work there anymore."

"So you ended up here," said the foreman, with a smile. "Is this fun?"

"Sometimes."

"It's work," said Aden as he rolled his cigarette. "It doesn't have to be fun."

Will shook out a loop and roped the bay as it backed away from the hay manger and tried to turn aside. The horse knew which animal he was after, and once he had it on the end of his rope, the game was over. Will dug in his heels to turn the horse, and then he walked toward it, coiling the slack.

Being the first one out to the corral again, Will did not hurry. As he patted the horse on the neck, he looked out across the rail to the horse pasture. He was barely able to pick out his own horse, the dark brown, in the twilight before sunrise, but he had a clear view of Ben Forrester's buckskin closer in. With the feeling that things were in their right places, he turned to walk the bay horse to the corral gate. He stopped short at the sight of Max Aden standing just inside the gate.

Aden was dressed as usual in his hat, denim jacket, and chaps. He had his rope tucked under his right arm as he pulled his gloves snug and flexed his hands. He showed no inclination to step aside.

Will moved forward. "Excuse me," he said when he was a couple of yards away.

"I've got a couple of words for you first."

Will stopped. "Say 'em, and let me get by. I've got work to do."

"I'll tell you this. You'd better watch your p's and q's."

The remark caught Will by surprise. He had made sure to keep out of all the banter and bickering the night before, and he had steered clear of Aden in every other way. He frowned as he said, "I don't know what you mean."

"You'd like to let on you don't know."

"Oh, shove along. I don't know what the hell you're talkin' about."

"The hell you don't."

"The hell I do, the hell I don't. You're just tryin' to pick another fight, and I'm not goin' for it. Let me by."

"You don't listen."

"About what?"

"I'm tellin' you to watch yourself. Don't put your nose in places it don't belong."

An image of Pearl flickered through Will's mind. It was the only thing he could imagine Aden was referring to, unless it was the conversations he had had with Jim Calvert, way off on the range. He knew Calvert wouldn't have said anything to Aden, even if he himself was a company man, and there was no way Aden could have been eavesdropping. No, it had to be Pearl. Blanche must have said something that had gotten around to Aden. But even at that, what was his motive? Aden didn't seem to have any interest in the girl—or in any Indian, for that matter—so it couldn't be jealousy. Beyond that, Will hadn't even gotten the chance to ask her anything in particular, such as about Ben Forrester.

"Well, I'll tell you," he said, looking at Aden. "I haven't been puttin' my nose in any place that concerns you. What I say or do is none of your business. So just let me by."

Aden stepped aside, and as Will went past, Aden tried the same trick he had used in the Lucky Diamond. He stepped on Will's spur, making him stumble and causing the horse to shy.

Will caught his balance and turned around as the anger surged up. He dropped his rope, and with both hands he grabbed Aden by the open jacket and slammed him up against the corral rails.

"Look here," he said, noting the surprise in Aden's muddy brown eyes. "We're not goin' to fight, not now, but I'm not goin' to put up with your maneuvers, either. Now if you want to fight and get us both fired, you can give it a try, but you can be sure I'll let Earl know how it got started. If you want to fight somewhere else, off the ranch, we'll do it fair and square. Meanwhile, follow your own advice and watch your own p's and q's." He relaxed his hold on the man's jacket and stepped back.

Aden's coiled rope slipped down to his right

hand, and he made a flinching motion as if he was going to raise it. Then his hand was still. "Stay out of my way," he said, with his voice tense.

"You stay out of mine."

Will gathered up his rope and slid the wooden latch on the gate. As he raised his head, he saw Jim Calvert and Brad Way, ropes in hand, looking on. Calvert had an amused expression, while Brad had the vacant look of a man who was waiting in line at the chuck wagon. Will pushed the gate open and walked through, raising his eyebrows as he handed Calvert the gate.

"Go on in," he said. "The water's fine."

Will took the horse to the hitching rail in front of the barn and went to work on him. The more he thought about the flare-up with Aden, the more he was convinced it was caused by his attempt at a few words with Pearl. He wondered if Aden heard about it directly from Blanche or from someone who heard it from her, like Ingram. More likely the latter. That could have been what had kept Aden in the cookshack the morning before, and then he took it upon himself to accost Will. Meanwhile, Blanche clamped down on her own, keeping Pearl out of sight. This was a tight bunch, but all they did was make him want to know more.

Chapter Seven

That evening at supper, Will felt that the atmosphere had lightened up somewhat. Donovan, all smiles, had called for Pearl to bring the coffee, and her glance had flickered once to meet Will's. Aden was silent, Ingram made his usual goodwilled comments, and Blanche moved back and forth without breathing fire and scorching the tabletop. Will could not get a sense of how closely these people shared their information, but he formed the general impression that the incident of his asking Pearl for bacon grease, so trivial in itself, had blown over.

A couple of minutes after Donovan left, Ingram took out his watch and wound it. "Boys," he said, "you can sleep in tomorrow."

The cigarette-rolling and pipe-stuffing came to a pause.

"That's right. Frank said you can have the day off."

Will had been keeping track of the days like anyone else, and he had noticed no mention was made the Sunday before. Donovan must have decided now that they were caught up enough to take a Sunday off.

"I won't argue," said Calvert.

Brad Way smiled. "Neither will I."

"Well, it was Frank's idea. You've got him to thank."

The foreman's tone made Will feel as if they were all orphans and the benevolent Mr. Donovan had left a shiny new penny under each of their plates.

"I wish I would've known earlier," Aden muttered. "I coulda gone to town."

"You've got all day tomorrow, Max. Get some rest."

Will smiled to himself as he finished rolling his cigarette. He had heard from Calvert that in addition to not smoking, Ingram did not drink. Perhaps to keep his men from going to town on Saturday night and perhaps to practice his usual method of not giving out information any sooner than he had to, he had waited until this late in the evening.

"Plenty of time for that later." Aden pulled the string of the Bull Durham sack with his teeth, and as he did so, Will noted that the man got in the last word whenever he could.

Will saddled his own horse in front of the barn, where the midmorning sun shone on its dark brown coat and warmed it to the touch. As he hadn't ridden the horse in over a week, he thought it would be a good idea to take it out. In addition, it gave a casual aspect to his going on a ride. No one had asked him what he was doing, and he hadn't said anything, but he took his time all the same.

He had the sense that someone was watching him, but no one else was in the ranch yard. As he looped his latigo and tightened the front cinch, he looked across the horse's back and caught brief glances at the ranch house, the cookshack, and the bunkhouse. He did not see movement at any window or door. Then, as he walked his horse out a few steps, Earl Ingram appeared at the bunkhouse door, leaned against the doorjamb, and raised his hand in a small wave. Will returned the gesture, then gathered his reins and mounted up. As he rode past the cookshack at a distance of ten yards, he saw a pale shape move back from the window a few feet. He was tempted to tip his hat, but instead he looked down at his horse's hooves as if he were watching how the animal stepped out.

Once he had crossed the first rise west of the ranch buildings, he turned his horse and headed northeast. He let the horse lope for about a mile, then slowed him to a fast walk for a half mile farther. Down in a swale where it looked as if a trickle of a stream ran for part of the year, he saw the remains of a sod cabin. The roof poles were gone and the walls were falling in. As he was in no hurry, he rode close to the ruins of the little shanty. On the west side, two cedar trees about four feet high looked as if they had reached their limit with no one around to water them anymore. They weren't in a place where they would catch any runoff or even have started on their own. A few yards farther out, a clump of parched wild rosebush stood at the head of a six-by-three area covered with pebbles and loose bits of sandstone. Feeling like an intruder, he touched his hat brim and rode on.

He figured it must be one of the places Ingram was talking about, although he could not see evidence of anyone trying to plant crops. More likely, someone had tried to make a go of it with a few head of stock and a quarter section, and after too many disappointments he had called it quits. Will imagined someone had carried water to those wild roses for at least a season. He wondered who was buried in that lonely place—a sad wife, a little boy who found a rattlesnake, a little girl whose fever wouldn't go away. If it was the man, the others probably wouldn't have stuck it out long enough to get the wild roses a start in their new place.

Will shook off the sad thoughts by recalling Ingram again. The foreman was a company man, all right, justifying whatever Donovan was up to in his buying up of smaller land holdings. For all Will knew, Donovan might have bought the parcel Will had just seen, or he might have his eye on it.

From what Will had seen and heard, an outfit that was buying up other claims usually concentrated on places with water, under the general principle that whoever controlled the water controlled the range. If a place was abandoned and dry, a man could run his cattle on it without paying a dime, although he might have to cut a fence or two. It was hard to say what kinds of places Donovan was trying to acquire. Maybe the man had a map and a checkerboard plan. People said the open range was coming to an end, and maybe Donovan had a vision of how to keep from getting fenced out of things he wanted or how to keep from having his free movement blocked between his own holdings. Will stopped his horse on a rise and scanned the country. All he could see was the wide, rolling surface that stretched away from him. Someone with a plan would have a map he could look down on, grids he could measure, points where he could center a compass.

Dunn Station came into view before the sun reached straight up. The building and corrals sat motionless in the full glare of the day, and the hitching rail showed no signs of Sunday visitors. Off to the left, a crow perched on the rail fence by the oil seep. Will took his horse on in at a walk.

When he had come within fifteen yards of the station, the front door opened and the proprietor appeared.

"Oh, it's you," he said.

"Sure is."

"I was wonderin' when I'd see you again. I heard you got on at the Redstone."

"Oh, did Max Aden tell you?"

Dunn's heavy brows went up. "No, he didn't. He don't come by here very much. And I don't miss him." With a glance at the horse, Dunn said, "Go ahead and water him if you like. You know where it is. Then come on in."

"Thanks." Will took the horse around back, let him drink about a gallon, and led him out front again to tie him up.

Inside the dim building, he looked in a corner to let his eyes adjust. Dunn was sitting in what was apparently his favorite chair, with his spit can at his feet.

"So what brings you here today? Are you on the job, or did that skinflint Donovan give you a day off?"

Will took a seat. "He let us enjoy the Sabbath."

"Hah! He's a good one." Dunn's dark eyes moved. "Can I get you anything?"

"If you've got any beer as good as the stuff we drank the other day, I could go for that."

"I'll let you be the judge on how good it is." Dunn rose from his chair and gave his trousers a hitch.

"Get yourself one, too."

"No objections to that."

Dunn went behind the bar and rummaged around. Will heard the tinkle of glasses, a cough from the bent-over proprietor, and then the dull sound of a full glass being set on the bar top. A moment later, Dunn came around the end of the bar with a glass of beer in each hand. He set them on the table and lowered himself into his chair.

Will raised his glass. "Here's to it."

"And them that can do it."

The beer tasted as Will remembered it, not cold but not flat.

Dunn set his glass down and smacked his lips, not quite as loud as before. "Well, what news from the Redstone?"

"Not much."

"Still nothin' on that young feller that got killed?"

Will shook his head. "No one seems to have an idea. The only one who's even talked about it has been Jim Calvert."

"Oh, he's all right."

"Sure seems to be. He's my workin' partner. We get along fine."

"That's good. At least you didn't get stuck workin' with Max Aden."

"I don't think that would have worked out very well."

"I heard you met him early on."

"You hear just about everything, don't you?"

Dunn shrugged. "What little news there is gets around."

Will took another drink, and his host did the same. Will brought out the makin's, troughed a paper, and shook out a narrow mound of tobacco grains. "Not much goin' on there," he said. "Ride out each day and check on things. We rounded up a few calves they missed on the first gather, but other than that we just go out in pairs and do the regular stuff."

"Four of you there now?"

"Four riders, then Ingram. Plus the cook and her helper."

"Oh, yeah. I heard they had a woman cook."

"Name of Blanche. Not a real friendly sort. And then there's an Indian girl helps her in the kitchen. Don't see much of her." Will rolled his cigarette and licked it, then smoothed the seam.

"Huh. It takes two women to feed five or six men?"

"I understand they had a bigger crew and just got rid of half of 'em."

"Jim Calvert could cook for the whole damn bunch. I guess he does, when they're out on the range."

"That's what he said." Will lit his smoke.

"Yeah. Donovan needs two women in the kitchen like I need Chinese chickens. If he didn't look so soft-petered, I'd think he was usin' one of 'em."

"I sure couldn't say."

"She probably kissed his ass and got him to give her a job." Dunn took out his tobacco pouch, pinched up a wad of stringy dark tobacco, and stuffed it in his left cheek.

Will laughed. "I have a hard time imaginin' that. She's a real harpy."

"Maybe that's what he needs."

"Anyway, that's the crew." Will thought it was just as well that he didn't say any more about Pearl. "And work's work," he added. He took a drag on his cigarette, lowered it, and turned it to see how it was drawing. He was pleased at having rolled a good even smoke.

"That's for sure."

"I could wish for a friendlier atmosphere once in a while, but the pay's reasonable and the eats are all right."

"What do you think of Ingram?"

"Oh, he's working for the company, that's for sure. But he keeps everything neat and organized."

"Never trust a man who doesn't drink."

"Or one who does. I don't suppose he comes in here very often."

"Every once in a while he'll stop in with the boys if they're passin' through. But he knows I don't like his boss, or his right-hand man Aden, and I don't pretend to. If I see him, it's usually somewhere else. Always civil, though."

"He's that." Will drank down the rest of his beer and set his glass on the table.

Dunn, who seemed to have been waiting, did the same. "Care for another?"

"You bet. Two more."

Dunn pushed himself up from his chair, gathered the two glasses, and went to the bar. Will smoked his cigarette and admired how evenly it was burning. After a minute or so, Dunn came back and set the two full glasses on the table. Easing into his chair, he leaned forward to reach his spit can, and at short range he made his deposit.

Will noticed smudges high on the man's sleeve as well as across the chest and belly of his shirt. As a way of changing the topic, he said, "I'd forgotten about that oil seep of yours until I rode up to your place again."

The man's dark eyes settled on him. "What about it?"

"Oh, nothin'. It's just somethin' interestin', somethin' I don't see or think about very much." Will raised his glass in salute and took a drink.

Dunn nodded and followed suit. "For the most part, it's just there."

"Not much of a moneymaker."

"Not now. But it could be."

"Oh, really?"

The man leaned on the table so that only the upper part of his shirt and suspenders was in view. A gleam came across his dark features, and he fixed his gaze on his visitor. "It could be the next big hurrah."

"Is that right?"

"Yep." Dunn cocked one eyebrow in a knowing expression, and it reminded Will of the way men acted when they wanted to allude to some great find of gold but didn't want to give away where it was.

"I would never have guessed."

"Look," said Dunn, in an almost-conspiratorial tone. "Men have been gettin' oil out of the ground in this country for damn near forty years."

"Here?"

"Well, they started in Pennsylvania, but they've been gettin' it at Fort Bridger for thirty years."

"I never knew that."

"A lot of men don't. And a lot of men don't know what it's used for." He left his comment hanging in the air.

"I don't know. Lubricate machines."

"That's one use. To lubricate steam engines and the axles on railroad cars. The other big use is for kerosene, a hell of a lot better than candles and a hell of a lot cheaper than whale oil."

"I see."

"But it doesn't take very many oil wells to fill all that need."

"I imagine."

"A few barrels go a long way to lubricate boxcar axles."

"Sure." Will finished his cigarette, dropped the butt on the floor, and ground it out with the sole of his boot.

"And furthermore, the cities are all goin' to electricity. You don't see anything but kerosene in the towns and ranches out here, but believe me, they're usin' it a hell of a lot less where there's the greatest amount of people."

Will took a drink of his beer. "This is all new to me."

"It is to most people." Dunn tipped his glass and drank more than half of what was left. "Now get this. They're drillin' *more* wells, not less."

"The hell."

"The hell yes." Dunn's face showed the animation of a prospector in full faith, and his voice held steady and low. "They've been doin' it for over ten years, just out in this country, that I know of. The first good one was well over ten years ago, at Dallas Dome. Now that's northwest of here. The more recent ones are around Casper. Now you ask, why are they doin' all this?"

Will blinked. "You bet I do."

In the same low voice and with his gaze leveled, Dunn said, "Because they believe it's the next big thing."

"When the demand is goin' down?"

"It's gonna go up!" Dunn opened his eyes wide and spit in his can again.

Will drew his head back and widened his eyes in return, but he said nothing.

"You know what an auto-mo-bile is?"

"Sure. They call 'em a horseless carriage."

"What do they run on?"

Will shrugged. "Steam, I guess."

"Some of 'em, but they're not doin' much. The ones that are comin' out, that are gonna be the next goin' thing, run on gasoline."

"Gasoline?"

"That's right. It's a by-product of petroleum. They used to just dump it out, until they discovered it made one hell of a good fuel."

"Not to make steam?"

"No. To replace it. It's a different kind of engine, and it burns the fuel inside. Not half as clumsy as a big steam engine on a little automobile."

"Well, that's something. I'd never have dreamed it."

"Most people wouldn't. You take the average man, and he wanders along starin' at the ass end of sheep—or like you, no offense, swattin' the hind end of a cow with your rope—and it's right there under his nose, all that time."

"Huh. And you knew about it when you took up this little piece of ground."

"You damn right I did. And every winter I go to Casper and get an idea of how far along things are going. One of these days someone'll come along who knows what's what, and he'll try to buy it cheap. And I'll be a step ahead of him, and if he's got the equipment, we can talk turkey. If he don't want to, I can wait for the next offer. I'm not goin' anywhere."

"How long do you think it'll be until there's a market?"

"Not long. They're makin' these machines right now. You'll even see 'em in Wyoming in a year or two." Dunn finished his beer and licked his lips. "Times are changin', boy."

"So I've heard." Will tossed off the last of his beer. "I believe I could drink another of those. What would you think of two more?"

"Just fine, and these are on me."

Feeling a glow of relaxation, Will rolled himself a cigarette as Dunn got up and fetched two more glasses of beer.

"Here," said the proprietor, setting a short, wide can on the table. "Helps keep the place clean."

Will lit his cigarette, shook out the match, and dropped it in the can.

Dunn spit into his own can and in a matter-of-fact tone remarked, "You don't have to repeat all of this, of course."

"No need to at all."

"None of it's secret, you know, but a man's business is his own."

"Sure."

"Just like you. You come here in the middle of the season, lookin' fer work, and that's all it is to me. A man lookin' fer work."

Will nodded. "And glad to find it, thanks in part to your recommendation."

"You didn't mention me, did you?"

"No, you said it wouldn't do much good, so I didn't bother."

"Just as well." Dunn rubbed his nose. "You say you don't mind workin' there."

"It's all right. Donovan's got a funny way of butterin' up everybody, and then Ingram goes on about what a swell place it is."

"Right in front of him, uh?"

"When he's there and when he's not."

"Like I told you, Donovan likes people to kiss his ass. I don't, and he acts like I should, but he don't pay my wages, so to hell with him."

"Have you ever had a run-in with him?"

"No, not at all. But a few years back, he was takin'

up a collection to hire a stock detective to come in here. He squeezed money out of a lot of these little operators, some of them are gone now, tellin' 'em that everyone benefited from the protection."

"Protection?"

"Against crime, he said. He even used that argument on me. I told him I didn't have any livestock and didn't need any protection against rustlers or whatever."

"I'd say." Will tapped his ash into the can.

"Then he said that if my customers benefited, I did. And it wasn't what he said, which was kind of ridiculous in itself, but the way he did it. You could say he leaned on me, tellin' me that if I didn't contribute to the protection I couldn't expect any."

"That doesn't surprise me. I suppose he leaned on all these little folks, too, whether they had livestock or not."

"Sure, and he still does, whenever he's got a mind to."

Will took a drink of his beer. "I understand he's trying to buy up a lot of these little places now. Has some investors who want to run a big herd of cattle, and he wants to get the grazin' for 'em."

"Could be. I've heard he picks up some parcels on auction, and he's never been shy about puttin' some pressure on one little fellow or another." Dunn tipped himself a healthy slug of beer. "I'll tell you, he looks like a soft-petered old bastard, but he's got plenty of drive left for pushin' other people and takin' what he can get."

"Does he do this by himself?"

"I think he trots his foreman and his young hothead around with him."

"I notice he packs his pistol, even when he doesn't need it." Will took a drag on his cigarette.

"Just practicin'. Gives him somethin' firm to get his hand around."

Will laughed and blew out his smoke.

"Anyway," said Dunn, "I don't have much to do with him. I don't go to his place, and he don't come to mine. He's another one that doesn't drink."

"Well, there's no drinkin' at the ranch, that's for sure, unless that woman Blanche keeps a bottle hid out. Probably just as well. Our friend Aden is cross-tempered enough when he's sober." Will looked at the ash on his cigarette. "Of course Jim Calvert, and that other fellow Brad Way, they're easy to get along with."

"Blanche. I bet that's somethin'," said Dunn.

Neither man spoke for a few minutes, and when it looked as if they each had one swallow of beer left, Will tried his question.

"Have you ever heard of a man named Al Vetch?"

Dunn pursed his lips and shook his head. "Nope. Is that what you're doin' here, lookin' for him?"

"Not at all. I've never heard of him, either. I just came here lookin' for work."

"I knew that."

Will took his time going back to the ranch, following a different route from the one he had taken on the way to Dunn Station. It was still early afternoon, and the beer left him feeling relaxed. His thoughts drifted to big cities, where electricity lit up the insides of buildings and where automobiles chugged in the streets. He gazed off to the north, where Dunn said men had been drilling for oil. It was a strange notion. He wondered how far below the surface the pools lay, and he wondered what they looked like. He imagined caverns with dark, shiny pools waiting to be tapped.

Twice out of the corner of his eye he saw a speck above the crest of a ridge, like the hatless head of a man, but each time as he turned to get a better view, the spot disappeared.

Back at the ranch, he unsaddled his horse and turned the animal out to pasture. He wondered if it was too late to get a bite to eat for dinner, but rather than go in and ask directly, he went into the bunkhouse.

Ingram was the only person there. He sat at the small table, wearing his snug vest but not his hat or gun. He was playing solitaire. After exchanging a greeting with Will, he reached for an envelope on the corner of the table and handed it forward with a smile.

"Thanks," said Will. He broke the seal and opened the envelope where he stood. As he unfolded the sheet of paper, he recognized the neat cursive handwriting.

Mr. Dryden:

I hope this letter reaches you all right. I am staying at the Continental Hotel here in town. I would appreciate seeing you when you get a chance.

Cordially,
Irma Welles

Will looked up from the note and met Ingram's inquisitive gaze. He tucked the letter back into the envelope and tapped the folded edge against his palm. "I just came back from a ride, and now it looks as if I need to go to town. Could I use a horse?"

"Sure." Ingram made a sincere expression as he nodded. "I hope there's no trouble."

"Oh, no." Will smiled as he tapped the envelope again. "Thorns on the rose."

Chapter Eight

Will took two steps out past the rear door of the bunkhouse and pitched the gray water from the basin. After peering at the little mirror inside as he shaved himself, he found the daylight almost blinding. He shook the tin basin a couple of times, took it inside, and hung it on a nail near the stove. Then he picked up the enamel kettle by its handle to take it back to the kitchen.

He knocked on the front door of the cookshack, as he had done earlier, thinking it was more diplomatic than just walking in when it wasn't mealtime. The door opened and Blanche stood there, no less flushed and no less imposing than before.

"Here," he said, holding the kettle forward. "Much obliged."

"Anytime." As she took the handle, her pale blue eyes gave him a looking-over, as if to see whether he had lied about the purpose of the hot water.

Will returned the favor, catching a glance at her full figure as she stood there. In spite of the wrinkles at the corners of her mouth and the sagging skin below her jawline, she had an insolent posture—a way of standing with her hips a little off center and slightly forward—that suggested an awareness of the body itself that some men would find her alluring. Who those men were, Will had no idea, and he did not think she was practicing on him. He was even more sure when she closed the door.

He did not waste time getting into a clean change of clothes, fetching a gray horse from his string, and saddling it. Tipping his hat toward the sun, which had passed the high point but was not yet slipping in the west, he rode out of the ranch yard.

The shadows in town were stretching when he found the Continental Hotel, which was a couple of blocks west and across the street from the Lucky Diamond. Thinking he would rather not signal his whereabouts, he found a stable where he arranged to have the horse watered, fed, and kept on hand until he should come back. He told the stable man he expected to be gone a couple of hours at most.

Inside the Continental Hotel, he saw the usual features of a hotel of its kind. Against the right wall, three empty chairs faced a stone fireplace that had a bare mantel. To the left of the fireplace, a dusty buffalo head stared straight ahead, while on the right, a set of deer antlers hung above an old muzzle-loading rifle. Straight ahead as Will walked from the door, the reception desk stood bare and simple with only the little brass dome of a bell. On the wall behind the desk, a pendulum clock in a case about two feet tall hung on the wall. The clock read a few minutes past four.

A man with a broad face and a high, shiny forehead came through a doorway next to the clock. "Yes, sir?"

"I'm here to see Mrs. Irma Welles, if she's in."

The man's eyebrows went up ever so slightly as he took a passing glance. "This way, please. Follow me."

To Will's surprise, the man went out past the end of the counter and led the way up a stairway. At the top of the stairs he turned right, walked with quiet steps on a carpet that occupied the center of the hall-way, and paused at Room 42. He knocked on the thin panel, and a few seconds later the knob turned and the latch clicked. The door opened inward, and there stood the smiling Mrs. Welles, very much as before.

"Oh, you were able to come," she said in a breezy voice. "How very good." With a nod at the hotel man she said, "Thank you."

As the man turned and made his quiet departure, Mrs. Welles said, "Please come in."

Will stepped inside and took off his hat, and as she turned to close the door, he took a quick survey of the room. Close to the door, along the right wall, sat a couch with a wooden frame and stuffed cushions. In front of it a low table squatted on an oval rug. Against the back wall stood a dark cabinet about chest high. To its left he saw a lighter-toned wooden chair. Beyond that, the left side of this ample room had the usual furnishings of a dresser, a washstand with basin and pitcher, an iron-framed bed, and a freestanding wardrobe with its doors closed. He did not let his eyes linger for very long on that side of the room, although there were no personal items in sight.

He stood with his hat in hand as she clicked the key in the lock and turned to face him.

"I hope you don't mind meeting here," she said. "I thought it would be better to keep out of the pub-lic view."

"It's fine."

"Shall I take your hat?"

"Sure." He handed it to her, and she hung it on a rack he had not noticed before, between the wardrobe and the door. As she did, he formed a renewed impression of her.

She was wearing the same outfit as on the last occasion, a light blue dress and a dark blue jacket. He imagined she didn't have a vast selection, and this must be the way she dressed for business. It also showed her figure to advantage, as she had a firm bosom and had not begun to pooch out at the waist.

She turned and smiled, showing her clean, even teeth. "Shall we sit down?"

"Fine." He turned to the chair that sat against the wall, lifted it, and set it near the corner of the low table so that it faced the sofa but not directly.

She sat on the sofa with her right arm on the wooden rest. "I'm glad you were able to come today," she said.

"It worked out all right. I hope I didn't keep you waiting, but I didn't get your note until I came in from a ride I had gone on."

"It's perfectly fine." Her face softened as she smiled again.

"You didn't have much trouble finding out where to write me, I guess."

"It wasn't very difficult. Everyone seems to know everything in this town."

"Except where Mr. Vee is."

Her eyebrows went up. "Oh, have you asked around for him?"

"Not much. Just with a couple of men whose confidence I think I can trust."

She let out a small sigh. "That's good." Then her face brightened. "Before we go any further, I want to give you this."

As she reached into her jacket pocket, he raised his head in expectation, hoping she would bring out a photograph. Instead, she produced a small purse with a beaded clasp, which she opened. She drew out a packet folded in plain brown paper.

"Here," she said, handing it to him.

He took it, felt its weight, and unfolded the paper. He counted five ten-dollar gold pieces. "I don't think I've earned this yet," he said.

Her face had a firm expression as she said, "I want you to take it now."

"Not wishing to argue, but our agreement was for fifty to begin with, fifty after a month or when the job was finished, and then something else if the job called for more. And it's been barely ten days."

"I know. But I thought I would give you this while I had it."

He wavered as he held the open packet in his palm.

"Please take it. Fold it up, put it away, don't look at it until the month's up, but please take it while I have it."

Will measured a deep breath, met the sincere look of her bluish gray eyes, and said, "All right. But I don't think I deserve it yet, and it should be enough for anything I have left to do."

"Don't think any more about it," she said. "Think about the work instead. Even if you haven't found out very much, I'm sure you have something to tell me." She sat poised, as if she were ready to take in information.

"Well, as you know, I got hired on at the Redstone."

"Was that the first thing you did?"

"Actually, no. I had to get my horse out of hock, get cleaned up, and travel here. On my way I met a man named Dunn who runs a way station, and he told me there might be a job at the Redstone. Then I stopped here in town, at a place down the street called the Lucky Diamond, and I got into a fight with a fellow who wouldn't leave me alone."

"Do you fight much?" She had an expression of light amusement on her face.

"More than I like, especially when it turns out that this little fightin' rooster works at the Redstone, too."

"And just for my information, what's his name?"

"He goes by Max Aden. He's one of those smaller men that's always out to prove themselves. I understand he's from Missouri, but from the way he talks and dresses, it sounds like he's worked in Texas."

She smiled without opening her mouth. "Certainly not Mr. Vee, as you called him, in disguise."

"I came to that conclusion."

"What else is there?"

"Well, even before I got to the Redstone, I found out there might be a job because one of the riders had gotten killed. And not by accident."

"Really?" She brought her eyes up to his, and he had the impression she had been looking either at his hands or at his six-gun.

"Yes, and that seems to be something else that nobody knows anything about."

"Sort of a mystery?"

"It would be more of one if anyone seemed willing to talk about it or inclined to solve it."

"That's odd."

"For the most part, they act as if nothing happened. Meanwhile, work goes on as normal, but I can tell things aren't right. So I figure, if I can find out what's going on there, it'll help me find the missing man. It's a hunch I have."

"It might be a good one." She shifted in her seat and then straightened up again with her forearm on the wooden rest. "Anything else?"

"I think so." Lowering his voice, he said, "The boss of the Redstone, an older man named Frank Donovan, seems to be buyin' up, or tryin' to buy up, various pieces of land in the area. This is where I thought the other fellow might come in. You said he'd done land-office work and that sort of a thing."

"He has."

"My thought is that Donovan might have him set up somewhere to take care of some of that work. Of course, he might be off in an entirely different place doin' somethin' else, and here I am lookin' under all the wrong rocks."

She gave a small shake of her head. "I think you're doing fine and should keep on doing the same thing for a while."

Will nodded. "Sounds all right with me." His hands moved, and he realized he wanted to roll a cigarette.

She must have caught something, for she said, "Mr. Dryden, can I offer you something to drink?"

"Well, um, I hadn't thought of it—"

She smiled. "But you wouldn't turn it down?"

He tipped his head. "No, I think it would be all right."

He watched as she rose from the couch, walked to the dark cabinet, leaned to open it, and brought out a full bottle of whiskey. She set it on top of the cabinet and took out two glasses.

"I believe I'll have a little myself," she said, "so you don't have to drink alone."

"Good enough."

She spoke over her shoulder. "By the way, I've got this room for a week, so if you need to get in touch with me, I'll be here. After that I plan to go back to Cheyenne to tend to things, and I'll be back in about two weeks from today. I'll get in touch with you again then."

He observed her shape as she had her back to him. "That sounds fine," he said.

She turned with two short, wide glasses, each one half-full. She handed one to him, set the other on the low table, and took her seat again on the couch. As he thanked her for the drink, her right hand went up to her light brown hair and brushed it back.

"You're welcome," she said. Then, after a pause, "Tell me more about the Redstone. Who knows what might be important."

Will took a sip of the whiskey, and the taste spread through his mouth. "Well, to begin with, there's the owner. I already mentioned him. Name of Donovan. He's about sixty, soft in the body and a little too smiling. Then comes his foreman, Earl Ingram, who's close to forty and straight as an arrow. After that we've got the four of us riders. I mentioned Max Aden. Then there's Brad Way, an easygoin' young fellow, and Jim Calvert, who's about Ingram's age and has been punchin' cows since he first learned to shave. He's the one I've got some confidence in."

"I thought you said there were two." She looked at him across the top of her glass as she prepared to take a sip.

"Oh, there are. The other one's Dunn, the fella with the way station."

"I see." The tip of her tongue was visible as she lowered her glass. "And that's the whole crew?"

"Well, there's the cook and her helper. White woman name of Blanche and an Indian girl." Again he was conscious of not saying much about Pearl.

He looked down at his glass and took another sip of the sweetish whiskey. "Like I said, I think there's something that's not on the square there, and since the person I'm looking for might be a little—"

"Go ahead."

"Well, in our last conversation you allowed me to think he was capable of doing things, shall I say, crooked."

She took another drink as well. "I allowed that, indeed."

"And you said he often goes armed."

"He does."

"So I figure, if there are a couple of things that don't look straight, he could easily be caught up in one of 'em."

She held her eyes level at him again. "Or both."

He flicked his eyebrows. "That depends on how crooked he is."

She hesitated, took another drink, and said, "Mr. Dryden, Al Vetch is as crooked as a dog's leg. Don't put anything past him."

He drew back. "I guess I won't." He took yet another sip and said, "I wonder how a nice woman like you would end up with someone like that. But of course that's your business."

"I'll tell you." Her voice had a quaver to it, as if the whiskey were taking effect, though Will thought it might come from anger. "He's a crooked son of a bitch, excuse my language, and I fell for it. He just wanted one thing."

"Oh."

"It's what his type wants."

Will shrugged.

"Money. What little I had, he wanted to squeeze me dry of every last penny."

Will sat wide-eyed.

"Does that surprise you?"

"Well, no, I guess not. I knew that some men put money ahead of everything else. I just don't think of that first when I think of what a man wants."

Her face had a hazy expression on it as she asked, "What do you want, Mr. Dryden?"

"Well, first off, I guess I just want to do what I set out to do, or how things have shaped up, and that's find the truth and find out what the connections are."

Her gaze relaxed. "Well, I think you're on the right trail."

"Like you said before, just keep doin' what I've been doin'. By the way, would it be all right if I smoke?"

"Sure. There's an ashtray in the cabinet."

As he went about rolling his cigarette, she got up, took a couple of steps to the cabinet, came back, and set a tin tray on the table.

"Thanks." He lit his cigarette, shook out the match, and dropped it in the tray. "Let me ask you a question if you don't mind, Mrs. Welles."

"Go ahead."

"What do you think this fella's up to?"

"Like I told you the other day, I think he's trying to raise some money so he can go somewhere else."

"Do you have an idea where?"

She paused and ran the tip of her tongue along the lower edge of her upper lip. "No, but I think I know with whom."

He held his cigarette in suspense. "Oh, really? Who would that be?"

Her eyes went steely cold. "The one he was with before. The tart who works in the kitchen."

His pulse jumped. "Not the Indian girl?"

"No, no. The white woman. The slatternly one."

"Blanche?"

"That's her. I thought she was off waiting some-where, but if she's in the picture here, then I imagine he's not too far off. I'd guess she got him some work with good Mr. Donovan. His kind of work."

Will let out a low whistle. "Then what do you want me to do?"

Her hand seemed to move in a careless motion as she raised her glass to her lips. After a sip she took the glass away and said, "Just keep doing what you're do-ing, like we said. As soon as we can find them to-gether, with witnesses, I've got what I need to keep him from ever coming back."

"Good enough." Will blinked, saw that he was close to the bottom of his glass, and finished it off. Then he raised his cigarette and took a long, leisurely drag.

"You look like you could use another drink."

He smiled at her through the haze of cigarette smoke. "I wouldn't turn it down."

"Good." She finished her own drink, stood up and held still for a second, and took the two glasses to the cabinet. A minute later, she stood with her hip not far from his shoulder as she handed him his drink.

"Thank you."

"My pleasure." She sat down again, shifted in her seat, and brushed at her hair. "What else?"

"Well, I don't know what else. I think I've got an idea of what might be up and what I've got to do."

"And what's that?" Her voice seemed to be drifting.

"Find Al Vetch," he said, feeling that he was re-peating the obvious.

"Oh, I'm sick of him. Sick of everything about him. Let's talk about something else."

"That would be all right. What about yourself?"

She waved her hand. "I don't want to talk about me. I feel like the biggest fool in the world. The girl who fell for it after everyone warned her."

"I don't know what else."

"Let's talk about you. Mr. Will Dryden."

He tasted his drink. It was whiskey, just like the last one. "We can do that," he said. "What would you like to know?"

She straightened up in her seat. "Why don't you come over here and sit down, so we don't have to shout at each other?"

"I could do that." He took another long drag on his cigarette, looked at the ash, and decided he'd gotten enough out of that one. He leaned forward and crushed the butt in the tin tray, then picked up his drink, walked around the table, and sat on the couch about a foot away from the woman. His motions seemed deliberate and slow to him, almost detached, and he had a faint memory of not having eaten anything since breakfast. He had drunk the beer in the meanwhile, and now this whiskey. But he was sitting next to a woman. He could get something to eat a little later.

"Well, Mr. Will Dryden," came the woman's voice. "What do you think?"

"What do I think of what?"

"Of this."

"Of what? Sittin' on a couch and havin' a drink?"

She peered at him. "Well, that. What else?"

He opened his eyes and let them relax. "Havin' a drink with a woman?"

"That's right." She held up her drink, he touched his to it, and they drank.

She ran the back of her fingers down the upper arm of his shirt. "Well, what about it?"

"About sittin' here havin' a drink with a woman? Why, it's all right."

"Just all right?"

"Well, no, it's better than that. It's a pleasure." He was pleased with himself for finding the words.

"You like it?"

"Sure. I like a drink. I like women."

She put her hand in his. "I thought you did. I thought you liked women."

He remembered the hand from before, not rough from work but not a soft lady's hand either. "Well, I do."

Her eyes were soft and her lips were moist as she turned to look full at him. "Do you like me?"

"Of course I do."

The dim afternoon swam around him as he lost himself in the kisses, the caresses, the pressing of their two bodies as they sprawled against the couch. Then her voice in his ear, "Big, strong Mr. Will Dryden," as he carried her to the bed.

He awoke in the dark. The woman was sleeping beside him. He could hear her breathing with her mouth open. Tangled memories came to him, a mélange of soft sound, turbulent motion, deep desire not held back. He imagined she had been wanting something like this for a long time; he knew he had.

She lay with her back to him. He knew he had to leave, but he wasn't going to just slip away. That was for other kinds of occasions. He laid his hand on her hip, and she stirred.

He rubbed her hip. "Kitten, I need to go."

"What?"

"I need to go."

She turned to him with the familiar smell of whiskey on her breath. He was sure his was the same.

As their lips drew apart, she said, "What time is it?"

"I don't know, but it's dark. I need to get back to the ranch."

She gave a long sigh. "Don't go yet."

"I have to go pretty soon."

She hooked her leg over his and drew him closer. "Pretty soon isn't right now."

He found his way to the stable, and after the fewest possible words with the man there, he led the gray horse into the night. The moon wasn't up yet, so he figured the time to be around ten or so. He hoped the ride back to the ranch would help clear his head. He took deep breaths and opened his eyes as wide as he could.

He was wrong. The moon was out. He just hadn't seen it because of the buildings. Now at the edge of town he could see it, a few days past a full moon, coming up in the dark sky.

A whistling, swishing sound brushed past his right ear. Something knocked his hat cockeyed, and the loop of a rope tightened around his upper arms. As the horse bolted from under him, his right foot hung up in the stirrup and then twisted free. He landed on his shoulder and hip, and as he sat up, someone leaned over and punched him in the face. The man leaned closer, loosened the rope, and tossed it aside. Then he kicked Will in the shoulder, the ribs, and the hip.

As the horse's hoofbeats retreated, Will knew

only a few things for sure. The man who had kicked him did not wear spurs and was too big to be Max Aden. The man who roped him was not the man who kicked him. It was going to be a long walk back to the ranch.

He stood up, found his hat, and felt himself in all the sore spots. Checking his pockets, he found the packet of coins from Mrs. Welles. None of that had been a dream.

Chapter Nine

Will jabbed the posthole digger down into the dark hole, pried on the two handles, and hauled up another load of dry dirt. He emptied the digger and plunged it down into the hole again.

His body hurt in every way he knew of—a headache from the hangover and hot sun, a stomachache from the greasy breakfast after almost a day of nothing but beer and whiskey, soreness where he had been punched and kicked, an ache in his feet from the long walk in boots, and now this pain in his arms and chest from digging in the hard white clay. Sweat poured down his face, spread across the front and back of his shirt, and made his pants stick to his legs.

He couldn't help thinking this was Ingram's idea of being clever, to send him and Calvert out to replace a fence corner at this time of year. It was much easier to dig postholes in the springtime when the ground was moist, and the dirt tamped in better then, too. As nearly as Will could see, there was no urgency to this task; it was just a grueling job for the hottest time of the year.

Jim Calvert stood tamping the previous post they had put in. "Hard and dry, isn't it?"

"You said it."

Will's shirt was soaked and had dirt clinging to it

when noontime rolled around. Calvert brought out the flour sack of cold meat and biscuits, and the two men began eating.

"I guess Earl thought it would be good for me to sweat it out," Will said," but it's going to take more than one day. The pit of my stomach feels like someone poured it full of acid and then gave it a kick."

"He just doesn't have any sympathy for a man who drinks."

"I wish it was just the drink. That would be bad enough, but it wouldn't be half of what I feel."

"Well, you had a few people guessing." Calvert opened his pocketknife.

"I imagine. What did they say?"

Calvert cut off a piece of gristle and tossed it away, then cut himself a bit of beef. "Earl said you came back in the early afternoon with drink on your breath and then went off to see a woman. None of us saw you in town, so Max said you must be laid up in a crib somewhere."

"Where was he?"

"He was in the Lucky Diamond. So were we. Brad and I left so we could get back before dark, but Max said he wanted a couple more. He came in after us, and I know it was dark by then."

"Before my horse showed up?"

"Oh, yeah. That horse came in after we went to bed. I heard the hoofbeats, and so did Earl. When you didn't come in to bed, he said he'd go take a look. He lit a lantern, and I decided to go along. I thought you might be out there in trouble, but all we found was the horse by himself, standing by the water trough."

"Was Max still in his bunk?"

Calvert waited to swallow. "I believe so. Why?"

"Well, before I even left town, someone roped me and jerked me off my horse. I admit I was a little stewed and didn't have my wits about me, but it was dark and I didn't expect a thing."

"What would they do that for?"

"So someone could hit me and kick me while I was on the ground."

Calvert frowned. "And you think it might have been Max?"

"Not the man who pounded on me. He was bigger. But whoever roped me made a good catch."

"You think there were two men?"

"I think so, but like I said, I was pretty woozy."

"I believe it. You stumbled around plenty when you finally came in."

"I had a hell of a time gettin' up this mornin'. I was lucky to make it to breakfast. What did they say about me before I got there?"

"Well, you know how Ingram is. He made it seem like he wasn't expressin' an opinion, but he said he thought you had enough to drink for a while. Then Max chipped in and said it was a pity a man had to drink so much that he fell off his horse."

Will forced himself to swallow the bite of dry biscuit. "Oh, he's a smart one. If he wasn't there, I bet he knows who was. I could feel him smirkin' at me."

"You think he could have been the one that roped you?"

"It's possible, as I think about it. They could have caught my horse and held it, given him a good head start, and then let it loose."

Calvert held his thumb against a chunk of meat as he brought his blade toward him to cut off a bite. "Well, I hope you got somethin' out of it to make you feel it was worth it, at least a little bit."

"I think I did."

"You don't remember."

"Oh, I remember. It's just that I feel so beat up and dragged out that I don't know what's worth it and what isn't."

Calvert laughed. "Well, you know Ingram has no interest in the drinkin', but I could tell he was a little resentful that you had a woman somewhere. Whether you did, of course, I'm not askin', but I could tell he was convinced of it, and I don't think he thought you deserved it."

Will smiled. "Maybe I didn't. But I don't think I deserved the rest of it, either." He reflected. "Well, maybe I did."

"Be that as it may, I still don't see the brilliance in pullin' us off our regular work to come out and do this for a day."

"Just to make me sweat as I dig holes. And to let you see it, I guess."

Calvert pursed his lips and watched his blade as he brought it through the chunk of cold meat again. "Well, like the old man says, all work is good work." He smiled wryly. "I guess it is, for either of them, as long as someone else is doin' it."

By midafternoon, Will's head began to clear enough that his thoughts didn't skip around, and he was able to think through his visit with Mrs. Welles. He did not think she had planned out the way things went. She did not seem that calculating, and her method was not that controlled. Had the act been premeditated as a way of keeping him inspired to follow through with his task, she not only would have been more careful with her own drinking, but she also could have saved herself fifty dollars. The more he thought about it, the more it seemed that she had planned the money as the incentive. He saw her more venturesome actions as impulsive, a yielding to temptation, aided by a few drinks and a desire to get even with a man who had run off, as she saw it, with a guttersnipe.

Will found it puzzling that a man would walk out on a woman like Mrs. Welles, who had her basic decency and intelligence, in order to mingle with a person like Blanche. Yet there was a logic to it, if he followed the reasoning in the right direction. People sought the company of others like themselves, and if Al Vetch had been with or lived with Blanche before, he was closer to her in nature than he was to the woman he exploited. He might be able to act the part in order to take advantage of her and her money, but he would revert to his true nature or level. As the old wisdom had it, what was in a person's blood would eventually show itself.

Up until this development, Will had had little more than the man's name to go on. Now, even though he had but the haziest image of the man's physical presence, he felt that he knew him better than before. The man with no face was a man with no scruples, crooked as a dog's leg, compunctious as a snake, comfortable as an alley cat with the blood that flowed in his own veins.

Will reined in his horse at the northernmost point in his ride. By his estimate, Dunn Station was less than two miles off. He could make it there and back, leave out riding most of his circle this one time, and not keep Jim Calvert waiting for long. With a small pang of guilt and worry, he put his spurs to the bay horse and set off at a lope.

A nondescript saddle horse was tied in front as

Will rode up to the station. The doorway was open, and Dunn appeared in its shadow. He was wearing his dark-stained brown hat, as if he had been outside and had just gone in.

"What do you know?"

"I was in the neighborhood, so I thought I'd drop in."

"That's fine." Dunn motioned with his stubbled chin. "Go ahead and water him. Then come on inside."

Will took the horse around the building to the trough. As he loosened the cinch and let the bay drink, he looked across the back area of Dunn's property and saw the fenced-in oil seep. Nothing stirred in the hot afternoon, and the sun reflected off the seep in dull black streaks. When he thought the horse had enough to drink, he took the animal around front and tied him.

Once inside the station, Will found Dunn and another man sitting at the table. They each had a low, wide tumbler with about two fingers of amber liquid in it, and they had an air of having suspended their conversation.

"Good afternoon," said Will.

The other man turned in his chair and nodded. He wore a sweat-stained hat and the clothes of a common ranchman or farmhand, and he looked as if had missed his weekly shave.

"Sit down," said Dunn. "I'll get you somethin'."

"Actually," said Will, looking at the table and not seeing an easy place to get a seat, "I didn't come for a drink."

"Just water."

Will assumed he meant the horse. "Well, not exactly that, either, though it's welcome once we got here."

The dark eyes roved over him and let up. "I don't know what else it would be. Castor oil?"

"No, I'm pretty well fixed for that, thanks."

"You've got me, then."

Will glanced at the stranger and came back to Dunn. "Maybe some tobacco."

"Oh, all right." Dunn pushed himself up out of his chair and walked, not without labor, to the other end of his establishment. He went behind the store counter and reached toward a shelf. "One or two?"

"I guess I'll take two."

Dunn set the pair of small white sacks on the counter. "Anything else?"

"Actually," said Will, with his voice lowered, "I was wondering if you heard anything about me."

Dunn raised his heavy eyebrows and gave a blank stare at the counter. "Nothin' new. Why?"

"Well, a little later in the day on Sunday, after I left here, I ended up in town. I had what you might call a business visit, and then someone surprised me in the dark and got in a few good licks on me. Since that was the day before yesterday, I thought you might have heard something by now."

Dunn shook his head. "Haven't heard a thing." He cast a glance in the direction of the man sitting by himself at the table. "We could ask Al."

"Al?"

"Oh, he's not any Al you ever heard of. Besides, you ought to meet him."

Will paid for his tobacco and followed the proprietor to the table. Dunn cleared his voice and remained standing.

"Al, this here is Will Dryden. Will, this is Al Stegman."

Stegman turned in his chair and nodded, very

much as before, and Will saw that they weren't going to shake hands.

Dunn sat down and rested his forearms on the
table. "Ah, don't worry, Al," he said. "He's all right."
Dunn looked up at Will. "When you first came in, or
that is, when you were waterin' your horse, I told him
who you were and who you worked for. He's got no
more love for the old bastard than I do, but I don't
think that'll bother you any."

"Not really."

"Just to give you an idea, Al." Dunn motioned with
his thumb. "This fella had a fight with Max Aden the
first five minutes he was in town. So he's not exactly a
company man."

Stegman made a small shrug.

The host directed his attention to Will again. "Al
here, like I said, doesn't admire your boss very much."

"Oh."

"Finds him pooshy."

"Sorry if you've had any trouble," Will offered,
but Stegman did not respond.

Dunn continued. "The boss of the Redstone is
tryin' to persuade him to sell out."

"Where's your place?"

Stegman half turned and said, "Out west of Popper Spring. A good ways from here, actually."

Dunn wagged his head. "Al comes here because
there's someone who shares his point of view. And
walls don't talk."

"That's fine."

"By the way, Al, have you heard about anything
that happened in town on Sunday?"

Stegman shook his head. "Nope. Haven't even
been there for damn near two weeks."

"Well, you don't have to go there to hear some-thin'." Dunn swirled his glass.

"I haven't anyway."

Silence fell for a few seconds until Will spoke. "How long have you lived out there by Popper Spring?"

"Three years. Long enough to prove up."

"And now he's tryin' to buy you out?"

Stegman's jaw lengthened. "Looks like he's doin' it."

"Well, I'm sorry to hear of it. A man works hard, and—"

"Mister, don't feel sorry for me, or even say you do. I know the kind of men he has workin' for him, and I know when it's time to go."

Dunn spoke again. "This fella's not that kind, Al."

"It doesn't matter. I'll take your word for it, but it doesn't make any difference."

Will did not feel comfortable keeping anything from Jim Calvert, but he decided not to tell him right away about his visit at Dunn Station. For one thing, he was shirking his work, and for another, his part-ner might well wonder if he had been sneaking off for a drink. There would be time to tell Calvert later if it seemed to matter enough.

Supper that evening was quiet. Donovan did not show up, and no one said a word about where he had gone. Will was used to the others not saying anything about the most obvious occurrences, and he made it a point not to ask questions around In-gram or Aden anyway, so he ate his supper without speaking. Afterward he went outside to smoke by himself.

He had it in his mind that sooner or later, if he loitered outside, Pearl would come to the front door of the cookshack. He did not know what gave him that notion, and he knew that it might be just a fancy, but he held on to the idea. He also knew that she would not come to the door while the other men were still inside, but he thought he should establish the pattern of going out and smoking by himself in the evening.

Supper went on without Donovan again the next night. The workdays and meals had taken on a quality of sameness, a quiet and uneventful continuum. As Ingram took out his watch to wind it, Will got up from the table, put his utensils in the pan, and went outside. He went across to the barn, where he rolled and smoked a cigarette.

Night fell, and the other men drifted out of the cookshack and into the bunkhouse. Will sat inside the open doorway of the barn, not lighting another cigarette because he did not want the glowing tip to show where he was. The door of the cookshack lay open, but he did not have a plan of what he would do if Pearl appeared. He thought that for the first time, if and when she did show up, he would not make his presence known.

He waited for a long time—somewhere between a half hour and an hour, by his estimate. Then a form approached the door. It was a silhouette because of the bright lantern light inside, but from the breadth of the shape he could tell it was Blanche.

She paused for a few seconds at the door and then stepped out. It looked as if she was carrying a lard pail in one hand and a gallon jug in the other. As she passed from the soft glow of light that poured from the doorway, Will could make out only the indistinct pale form moving away in the darkness.

He thought she was headed to the ranch house, which had no light showing in any of the windows. Glad he had left his spurs in the bunkhouse, he rose from his seat and moved with quiet steps along the front of the barn. The form was still moving diagonally across the yard, in the direction of the little stone structure he had taken to be a springhouse. No light appeared there, either.

He moved along the outside of the corral, some fifty or sixty yards behind Blanche. He thought she came to a stop, so he stopped. He heard a muffled rapping sound, a voice, the click of a latch, and then the scrape of a door opening. A ray of light spilled out for a moment and then closed off.

He was sure he had seen a couple of windows in the little stone house during the daytime, and now he supposed they were blocked out. But there was sure enough someone in there. Will let out a long breath. He could kick himself. Here he had been at this ranch for ten days, looking for a man who was right under his nose.

Will made himself stay calm as he tried to think things through. Blanche had taken the man food and water, but there was no telling how long she might stay. It was hard to know what to do—whether to draw close to the building and try to catch some of the conversation, or whether to take advantage of the moment and try to talk to Pearl. Hoping that Blanche would stay in the little stone house for a while, Will crossed the hard-packed yard. As he did, he searched the entire form of the ranch house as it loomed on his left, and again seeing not even a crack of light, he took long, quiet steps toward the cookshack.

As the door was still open, he walked on in. He was glad to see no one in the mess area. A clatter of dishes told him someone was in the kitchen, so he went there, letting his feet fall normally so that he wouldn't seem to be sneaking. Just as he arrived at the kitchen doorway and could see her, Pearl turned and gave a start.

"Hey," he said in a low voice. "I didn't mean to scare you."

She took a close breath as her dark eyes moved over him. "Do you need something?"

"I'd like to talk to you if I could."

She frowned in the direction Blanche had gone. "I don't know if I should."

"Don't worry. I won't do you any harm. I'd just like to ask you about a couple of things."

He noticed the perspiration on her brow as she dried her hands on her apron. She was wearing a dark gray cotton dress that showed dampness on the shoulders and across the back.

"I don't know." Her eyes seemed to be searching him.

"Just for a few minutes. We can go out back where it's cooler, and if someone comes, I'll take off."

She wiped the back of her hand across her brow. "All right."

Outside, the night air felt fresh. No noise came from the bunkhouse or any place else in the ranch yard, but he knew that either Blanche or one of the hired hands could show up at any minute.

"Over here," he said, leading the way to the corner of the cookshack farthest from the bunkhouse and the outbuildings. Enough moonlight showed so that he could see her face and bright eyes.

"What is it?" she asked in a voice just above a whisper.

"I don't want to get you in any trouble, but I'm trying to find out about a couple of strange things that have gone on around here."

"Well, I don't know anything."

"I think you can help me. Whether you can or not, if I can help you, I will. Do you believe me?"

"I don't know. I guess so."

"Good." He went to touch her for assurance and decided not to. After a few seconds of searching for words, he said, "Look. I know this is something no one here wants to talk about, but I would like to know about Ben Forrester."

"What about him?"

"Well, first, why anyone would want to do something to him."

Her face slipped from view as she looked down and away. "I don't know."

"You were friends with him, weren't you?"

"We talked."

"Jim Calvert tells me Ben was kind of sweet on you. There's nothing wrong with that, but it's true, isn't it?"

Now her eyes were visible. "Ben was a very nice boy. He cared about me and said nice things."

"And you cared about him?"

She looked away. "What does it matter?"

"Look," he said. "Anything you can tell me can help."

"I don't know anything else."

"Let me put it this way. Do you think anyone was jealous of him? Maybe someone who also liked you and didn't like to see him coming around?"

"I don't know what other people think."

"Not Max?"

"Oh, no."

"And not Earl, or Brad, or even Jim?"

She did not answer right away, but her voice sounded decisive when she said, "I don't think so."

"How about Frank? Mr. Donovan?"

She shook her head. "I don't know."

Will tried to speak in a matter-of-fact way. "In just the little bit I've seen, he seems to like you."

"Oh, he might."

"But he's never done anything about it?"

"Like what?"

"Oh, I don't know. Try to get you off alone. Touch you."

"No, nothing like that. I always think he might, but he hasn't. And like Blanche says, he's an old man. What could he do?"

Will did not like to think about that enough to give her an answer. Instead he said, "So you don't think he was jealous enough to have someone take Ben out of the way?"

She shook her head again. "No, I don't."

"Has he acted different at all? Any more forward, for example?"

"No, not really."

"So he might be a little jealous, but not that much."

"That's what I'd say."

Will took a breath and steadied himself. He felt that time was racing, yet he didn't want to rush through and then wish he hadn't. "What else do you know about Ben—that is, what else that might give me an idea of why someone might have something against him?"

"Like what?"

"Well, people get killed because someone else is

jealous, or wants to get even, or doesn't want them to say something. Those are just examples. There's also money, but that doesn't seem to have anything to do with this here."

"No, it doesn't."

"And no one had a reason to get even with him for anything?"

"I don't know."

"Or wanted to keep him quiet about something?"

"I don't know that, either."

He did not think she was being difficult, but he did not feel he was making enough progress, either. "I think it might be something like that," he said.

"It could be."

"Can you think of anything—anything at all that he mentioned or seemed worried about?"

She moved her head back and forth, and he followed the shine of her eyes. "Not that I can remember, but he did seem worried. He just didn't say why."

Will narrowed his eyes as he tried to sort things. "Did he ever mention knowing a Mrs. Welles?"

"No. Who is she?"

"If he didn't know her, it doesn't matter, and I don't think he did. I think at some point she might have hired an investigator, but I don't think it was Ben. Things don't match for that. What about this man named Dunn, who runs the way station? Did you ever hear him mention that name?"

"No."

Will was trying to think of a way of phrasing a question about Al Vetch when the back door of the cookshack jerked inward and a glow of light fell on the ground.

"Pearl!" shouted Blanche in her coarse voice. "Where are you, girl?"

Will ducked out of view behind the corner of the building as Pearl took a couple of steps toward the outhouse.

"I'm right here," she said in a strained voice.

"What in the hell are you doin' out here? Who else is there?"

"No one." Pearl had her hand on her stomach. "I just have a lot of wind in me."

"You girls. You want to faint with your monthly sickness."

"But it hurts."

"Well, let it out, and get back in here. I can't do everything myself."

Pearl walked toward the light and out of Will's view. He heard her go up the wooden step, and then the door closed and left the night in darkness.

Chapter Ten

The sun had not yet risen when Max Aden, in his sullen manner, rode out of the ranch yard without saying a word to his partner. Will, who was already mounted up and waiting for Jim Calvert, watched without thinking as Brad Way finished pulling the cinches on his own mount and swung up into the saddle. Then, as the young man was going through the routine of adjusting his reins and trying to catch his right stirrup, the roan horse started bucking.

Will tightened the reins on his horse and waited to see what the roan was going to do. The animal bucked forward and back in a rocking motion, which was not likely to throw a good rider except that Brad had lost balance and was leaning to his left. Then the horse switched ends, and Brad came up straighter. He dug with his right foot, not to spur the horse into bucking more, but to try to stay upright. The horse switched again and went back into its rocking motion, landing on its front feet and kicking with the hind ones. Will thought Brad was going to ride it out all right until he saw that the roan was moving over to the corral and was probably going to try to rake the rider off on the rails. To complicate things, Brad's right spur had caught in the strands of his cinch, making it hard for him to keep his balance or to jump if he wanted.

Will spurred his horse forward, dead at the corral and in the path of the bucking animal. Will's horse stopped as he hoped, bunching its hind quarters under it and bracing itself against the roan, which must have been surprised at being pinned against the corral. Will grabbed the headstall near the bit and pulled down, settling the animal's motion to a little dance and then stillness.

"Thanks," said Brad, looking down as he unhooked his stirrup from the cinch. "Sumbitch wanted to buck a little bit." He raised his head and smiled. "We'll give it another try." With his foot in the stirrup and his reins set, he nodded.

Will turned his horse back to the ranch yard as Brad let the roan walk out. Max Aden had turned his horse around and was waiting, gloved hands on the pommel. As Will reined his horse and turned further, he saw Earl Ingram a few steps out from the cookshack, hat in hand. Pearl was standing in the doorway.

Jim Calvert, who had mounted up by now, rode alongside Will. "Good move," he said.

"Thanks. Made a little commotion, looks like." Will nodded to Earl Ingram and then exchanged a glance with Pearl. Her face didn't show much expression, but he thought he saw approval there.

The morning's ride took Will and Calvert to the northwest of the ranch. By now, Will had a familiarity with many of the large draws he passed, although it seemed as if every once in a while he would come across an unfamiliar gully or canyon where he was sure he had ridden before. It was as if the land opened and shifted, although he knew it didn't.

He also began to recognize some of the cattle, most often cow-calf pairs, as those were the ones he had been on the lookout for earlier, but also steers, yearling heifers, and bulls. In addition, he recognized some of the cattle carrying other brands. All of these open-range animals were half-wild, so he kept his distance and they kept theirs. He continued to look for anything irregular, such as an influx of cattle with another brand or an uneven distribution of animals over this sparse grazing area. But the whole vast range seemed uneventful and unchanging.

He did make one small discovery, which was not startling to a range rider. Down in a dry wash, in a spot that was not visible except from the ridge above, he found a dried and wrinkled cowhide. Most of the reddish brown hair was still on the hide, and the head was attached. Will took it to be a young animal, a year or a little better, and he figured this was some of last winter's activity. Knowing it was the custom for a cattleman to eat anyone's beef but his own, he thought this might even be the work of some of Donovan's men. For someone like that, though, it was easier to herd an animal back to the ranch than to pack it, especially if it had a distant brand. A homesteader, on the other hand, might have taken this opportunity and might have availed himself of a smaller animal because it was easier to cut up and haul. Whatever the case, it was old work and the meat was long gone.

At midmorning, Will met up with Calvert on a rise overlooking a wide, desolate flat with no cattle in sight. As usual they dismounted to get a little rest from the saddle and to share observations.

"Things look pretty much the same," said Will as he rolled a cigarette.

"Slow time of year. Calves grow, cows fatten up a little. But there's not much change from one week to the next."

"Saw one old hide tucked away in a gully. Looked like somethin' from last winter."

Calvert sat with his hat back on his head, looking as if his only concern in the world was getting the loose strands of tobacco into the bowl of his pipe. "Prob'ly," he said.

"I met a fellow at Dunn's place the other day," Will said, thinking that it wouldn't hurt to collapse the two visits into one. "Name of Stegman. Said he had a place over west of Popper Spring."

Calvert pursed his lips. "He wouldn't have to come this far for beef. Could be anybody's work."

"Oh, I know. It just put me in mind of him." Will lit his cigarette and handed the match to his partner.

"Uh-huh."

"He seemed a little down in the mouth."

"He always does. He's got one of those faces that're called downers. I worked with a fella like that. His name was Dan. They called him Downer Dan." Calvert puffed a rich cloud. "Not a pleasant name. Better than Horse Thief Huntoon, though. Knew a fella who was called that, too."

"Not to his face."

"No, and he died in a brothel."

"With his boots on?"

"As I heard it. People were surprised there wasn't whiskey runnin' out of the bullet holes."

Will took a puff on his cigarette. "Why can't folks learn to get along?"

"I don't know. Damnedest thing."

After a pause, Will continued. "This fellow Stegman says he's plannin' to pull up stakes."

"Oh. Had enough?"

"From what he said, I understood he'd had enough of being pushed on by one of his neighbors."

Calvert made a long face. "Someone not totally unconnected with the Rafter Six brand."

"As I understood it."

"Well, I'm not surprised. He's gotten to several of 'em, little by little."

"Has he been doin' this for a long time, then?"

"I'm not sure how long. This is only my second year here, so I don't have much of the history."

"But you say he's been here about ten years."

"Something like that."

"Well, you see a case like this one, even if the fella's a downer like Stegman seems to be, and you can't help thinking."

"Always gets a man in trouble, thinkin' does."

"Yeah, but you do it yourself."

"Oh, sure. That's how I know it can get you in trouble."

Will looked at his ash and took another drag. "Makes you wonder how square this whole deal is about the foreign investors. For one thing, if they so much as sent one rep out here, they'd see there's a lot better grass to be had elsewhere." He waved at the plain in front of them.

Calvert puffed. "Oh, yeah. Like I said before, I've never seen any of these investors or anyone representin' 'em."

Will plucked at the short, dry grass on the ground in front of him, hesitating but knowing he needed to go further. "I'll tell you," he said, "I heard something from Dunn himself that was interesting."

"If it was about the boss of the Redstone, it wasn't very flattering, I'd bet."

"Well, that too. But this was about something else."

Calvert gave a wry smile. "The evils of drink?"

"No, he didn't quite get to that. What he talked about was oil."

"I suppose he knows somethin' about it, havin' a wallow of it right next to his place."

"He seems to. He says he's been keepin' up on the subject. Most of it's new to me, but if there's anything to it at all, it could be big doin's."

"Like how?" Calvert tamped his pipe with the empty shell casing, wiped the brass on the knee of his trousers, and slipped it back into his vest pocket.

"Well, he says they've been gettin' oil out of the ground for years, back East and out here."

"I believe that's true."

"And he says one main use has been for lubrication—machines, especially steam engines, and things like railroad car axles. And the other main use has been for kerosene."

"I think all of that's pretty straight, too, from what I've heard."

"Then he says the demand for kerosene is goin' down because people in the cities are usin' electricity, which is cheaper and brighter."

"Probably safer, too. Remember the Chicago Fire."

"Right. But then he says that in spite of the demand goin' down, people are drillin' more wells. He says they've been drillin' 'em north of here, up around Casper and thereabouts, for ten years."

"I've heard some of that, too."

"And do you know why, accordin' to him?"

"No, I don't. I'd heard about the oil, but not about why."

"Accordin' to Dunn, who says he goes to Casper

every winter to keep up on the news, there's a new demand, or there's going to be."

Calvert puffed again and nodded. "All right."

"It's gasoline. He says it's something they used to throw out but they discovered it makes good fuel."

"For heating?"

"I don't know about that, but he says it's to run a new kind of engine. For automobiles. Not nearly as clumsy as a steam engine."

"Well, I'll be damned."

"These automobiles are already out, of course."

"Sure. I've heard of 'em."

"He says there'll be one in Wyoming in a year or two."

Calvert's eyebrows went up and down. "Might as well. A place like Cheyenne is already full of bicycles. And he seems to know what he's talkin' about."

"If he just heard it from other people passin' through, I'd have my doubts. But he goes and finds out about it."

"Could be. I thought he went there for the whore-houses."

"Maybe he does that, too. But he gave me the impression that there were some men who knew what they were doing, and he's been onto it for a while."

Calvert's eyes opened. "So that's why he bought that place."

"I think so. He's just sittin' on it, waitin' for the opportunity."

"Well, what do you know." Calvert chuckled. "He's like that woman who said, 'I've been lookin' for a pot of gold all my life, and here I find I've been sittin' on it all this time.'"

"She wasn't a biscuit shooter."

"No."

Will took a long breath. "And here's my next thought. If Dunn has known about it all this time, and it's no secret, just somethin' that your average cowpuncher or sheepherder doesn't know much about, then chances are that the boss of the Redstone has been workin' on a similar idea."

Calvert pushed his mouth up into a thoughtful pose. "That could be. Let on that he's gatherin' up poor rangeland at hardscrabble prices—nickel, dime, fifteen cents an acre. As long as no one knows the real motive, they might sell out pretty easy."

"And even if someone does, like Stegman seems to, he might yield to the pressure anyway."

"Whew. Did Dunn tell you all this when Stegman was there?"

"No, it was earlier. But I got the sense that he knows about it. He and Dunn act as if they have a lot of shared knowledge between 'em."

"They likely do."

"So I think Stegman's been pushed pretty hard. He's bitter about it, but he says he knows when it's time to go."

Calvert shook his head. "Well, that's an ugly way. It's one thing to take advantage of an opportunity or of other people's ignorance, but it's another thing to chisel and threaten."

"That's how I see it."

After a moment of silence, Calvert clucked his tongue. "Sons of bitches. You try to do your job and not know things, and yet you know better all along." The wrinkles showed at the corners of his eyes as he looked straight at Will and said, "I don't know about you, pard, but I've quit better outfits because I didn't like some of the company I kept there. Come the end of this season, I think I'll roll my blankets and look for another range."

"Me, too, if I last that long," said Will, crushing the stub of his cigarette. "I expect to get fired every day."

"Ah, they need someone, and Earl's not going to ride out every day himself."

"I believe that." Will gazed across the empty country again. "I'll tell you, there's one other part to this that I haven't made sense of."

"What's that?"

"What happened to Ben Forrester."

Calvert lowered his pipe. "If I thought he was crooked, I wouldn't give it much thought. I'd figure someone got him for somethin'. But I think Ben was as straight as they come."

"And it doesn't seem like anyone would do it out of jealousy."

"Nah. That wouldn't be strong enough." Calvert held up his hand with his index finger crooked downward.

"The only other think I can think of is that he knew somethin' that someone wanted to keep him quiet about?"

"Such as?"

"I have no idea. I don't think it could be this land scheme, whether it's for poor grazing land or the oil underneath. Even if not many people around here know about oil, it's not a secret, and not something to kill someone over."

"I'd go along with that. Men will kill for land and property, but as far as I know, Ben didn't have any. They'll kill to protect deep, dark secrets, also, but I don't see one here."

Will stared at the landscape. "I don't, either. But I

do know you can have something right under your nose and not see it." He felt a strong temptation to tell Calvert about the little stone house and who he thought was in it, but he resisted. For one thing, he didn't want anyone to know that he knew, because as long as he and Calvert and Brad Way seemed not to know, Al Vetch was probably not going anywhere. Donovan would keep him out of sight so that he would never be a suspect for anything that came up. The way Will saw it, he had to come up with a plan for getting some proof, some tangible testimony, that Al Vetch and Blanche were together. That would be the end of his job for the missus, and then he would see if there was a way to connect the hidden man with the death of Ben Forrester. For the time being, it was as if he had Al Vetch on ice, but he knew it wouldn't last long.

Calvert spoke. "Isn't that the truth? It's like this oil."

"It sure is. Dunn said the same thing. That's probably what made me think of it."

Blanche held her head back and to one side as she set the steaming pot on the table.

"Stew," said Ingram, raising his chin. He took the bowl that Calvert handed him and ladled the mixture of meat, potatoes, and onions into it. "Here you go, Frank." He set the bowl in front of the boss of the Redstone, who gave his bland smile and a vague nod to anyone who might be looking.

Blanche returned with two plates of biscuits, set them down, and left.

"Speakin' of stew," said Ingram, "we had an Irishman for a cook, out in Idaho, and he made mutton stew. He'd get a sheep and hang it, especially in the fall, and we'd have mutton stew every day for two weeks. I can still remember the taste of it, and the greasy smell."

"This is beef stew," said Donovan, pausing with his spoon.

"Of course it is. Now you could eat this every day and not get tired of it." Ingram served himself a bowlful and turned the handle of the ladle around to Calvert. "Spuds and mutton. That old Irishman was full of stories about how they skinned their sheep and boiled their spuds. Work the hide off with their fist. I saw him do it one time, and he got that grease all the way up to his elbow. And then the spuds. He said they had a big open tank, back in the Old Country, where they boiled potatoes for the hogs—all the bad ones, you know—and there was a widow and her kids used to come and eat out of there." Ingram held the biscuit plate toward his boss.

"Poor people," said Donovan, taking a biscuit.

"That's right, and this was before the famine. Watson said it got worse. That was his first name, by the way. Watson. I don't remember his last name. It might have been O'Connor."

"That's an Irish name. Donovan is, too, but we came over a lot earlier."

The ladle came to Will, and he served himself some stew.

Ingram had not begun to eat and seemed in no hurry. "Sure," he said, nodding to the boss. "Another story he liked to tell was about racing dogs. You know, in the dog races they use rabbits or hares, but these common people, when they were trainin' the dogs, used cats. Of course, the cats would run up a tree, so they never got to train 'em for a very long stretch. Anyway, one day a couple of these fellas entered their dogs in a race, and it was a foggy day. As soon as the rabbits took off, the dogs lost 'em in the fog, and instead of followin' their trail, they ran over to the nearest tree and started barkin'."

Donovan gave his little laugh. "Barkin' up the wrong tree."

Brad Way finished serving himself and moved the pot toward Aden, who also seemed inclined to talk.

"Those would make good coon dogs," Aden said.

Ingram half frowned. "Wonder if they have coons there. I know they've got foxes."

Donovan came back into the conversation. "When I was a boy we had a coon for a pet. Back in Illinois."

"They make good pets," said Ingram. He put his spoon into his stew.

Aden answered. "They turn on you when they get older. 'Specially an old boar. I heard of one that chewed his owner's ear half-off. Had to kill it. Could've saved himself some trouble and done it a lot sooner."

Donovan called toward the kitchen. "Is the coffee ready?"

Conversation lapsed at the table as the biscuits went around and the men began to eat. Pearl appeared with the coffeepot and waited near Donovan's elbow. Will had formed the impression on earlier occasions that the boss liked to keep her hovering there, and it seemed to be the case now.

"Speakin' of pets," said Donovan, without glancing at the girl, "we had a fawn antelope the first year we were on this ranch. Had the prettiest eyes. The men called her Elsie. She stayed all through the summer, and then she was gone." He turned a coffee cup right-side up and said, "Here."

Pearl poured the coffee and set the pot on the table.

As she did, her eyes met Will's, and they seemed to say, *I am not part of this*. Then she stood straight up.

"Thank you, Pearl," said the boss. He turned his head to watch her walk away. As he did, Will thought his gray hair looked too perfectly in place.

After supper, Will went to the bunkhouse with the other men. He imagined Blanche would be on the lookout to see if anyone tried to talk to Pearl, so he thought he would let her keep watch in vain this evening.

Brad Way had shaved off all the bark from the stick of chokecherry wood, and now he was trimming the rough patches and smoothing the surface.

Ingram, who seemed more talkative than usual this evening, said, "What do you plan to do with that stick, anyway?"

"I don't know," said Brad. "Just somethin' to fool around with."

Ingram shifted the toothpick beneath his full mustache. "At first I thought you were just tryin' to see how long you could get the strips you were shavin' off."

"Mostly I'm interested in seein' what kind of wood it is."

"Not very good, really. Kinda soft. Not much good for firewood. People use it to make an ax handle or a shovel handle, but it bends on you when you use it, and a good part of the time it splits when it dries."

Aden spoke up. "Short piece like that, you could use it for clubbin' animals in a trap."

"Your better ax and shovel handles," Ingram went on, "are made of ash or hickory. Something harder. None of that grows around here, of course, so if someone's in a tight or just downright broke he'll use chokecherry. He'll have to look around to find one big enough or straight enough. Isn't that right, Jim?"

Calvert did not look up from the game of solitaire he was studying. "Oh, yeah."

"Most of the wood in this country is soft. Cottonwood, pine."

"Cedar's tough," said Calvert.

"That's true, but it's not good for ax handles. And it takes a hundred years for one to grow big enough to be a fence post."

Max Aden, restless as always, got up from his bunk and went to stand by the front door as he finished smoking his cigarette. The top of his head with its receding hairline showed pale from the last light of the evening, and his deep-set eyes seemed to be searching the ranch yard for something he could disapprove of. He pinched the tiny stub of his cigarette and threw it outside.

Calvert spoke up. "Not bad firewood, though."

"What's that?" said Ingram.

"Cedar."

"Oh. Uh-huh."

Silence grew in the bunkhouse for the next few minutes. Ingram cleared his throat and shifted in his chair. Aden rolled another cigarette, lit it, and tossed the dead match outside. Calvert gathered up the cards and began shuffling them.

Finally Brad Way spoke up in the general tone of making conversation. "I wonder who's looking after Dunn's place."

Will could feel the dead silence.

"Why's that?" asked Calvert as he cut the deck.

Brad looked at Ingram and then Aden. "Well, because of what happened."

Calvert paused in his shuffling and glanced around. "What happened?"

Brad hesitated until Ingram gestured for him to go ahead. "Well, old Dunn got killed earlier this afternoon."

"The hell," said Calvert, sitting straight up and frowning. "How did you know about it?"

Brad looked at Ingram and Aden again and said, "Earl told us when we came in."

Calvert moved his gaze from Will to the foreman. "We didn't hear anything about it."

Ingram's blue eyes held steady as he shrugged. "I guess I didn't think of it. I probably thought it would just come out in conversation, and you can see it did."

Will's face tensed. So that was what the talk about mutton stew and race dogs was all about, just to keep this other topic at a distance.

Calvert turned to Brad Way. "Earlier this afternoon, you say."

"That's right. Earl can tell you."

Ingram shook his head. "Nah, you're doin' fine. You know as much as I do, anyway. I told you everything I heard from the sheriff's man."

Brad's eyes shifted around, and Will could tell he didn't like being put in the position he was in.

"Well," said Calvert, "is there an idea who did it? Any witnesses?"

"I don't know. That fella Al Stegman found him. He got questioned."

"They don't think he did it, do they?"

"Probably not. He said he was friends with Dunn."

"Good chance of that. What else did he say?"

Brad looked even more uncomfortable than before. "He said he could prove it."

"Oh."

"He said Will Dryden had just been there at Dunn's place on Monday, and he, Will, could testify that Stegman and Dunn were friends."

Calvert and Will exchanged a glance, and then they both turned to the two company men. Ingram had taken out his knife and was cleaning his fingernails, while Aden was holding a cigarette to his lips and staring out into the dusk.

Chapter Eleven

Will studied the land to the west of him as the sun warmed his back. The news of Dunn's death was still sinking in, as was his awareness that Ingram had let him and Calvert find out on their own. Meanwhile, the daily routine went on as before, as if nothing had happened. After breakfast, Ingram had sent the riders out on their usual rounds and had made no further comments about Dunn.

As for suspicion, the visible men at the Redstone were all in the clear. Will and Calvert had been out riding together and could easily vouch for one another. The same went for Max Aden and Brad Way. Donovan had come back to the ranch before noon dinner, and Will remembered that the boss had showed up at the cookshack as the four riders were leaving. He and Ingram, according to Brad, had sat at the table for two or three hours, discussing the business of the ranch. Not long after that, a sheriff's man had come by with the news and had left with a satisfactory account of where the hired men had been working.

What the sheriff or his man would not think to ask about, of course, would be a person they did not know existed. It seemed like a bold maneuver, but Will could imagine Al Vetch going out in the clear light of day, when everyone was occupied and out of the way. It would have been a quick job to take care of Ben Forrester and a little more time-consuming to go to Dunn Station, but a man could do it. The question of why still remained, and Will knew he was not going to find an answer in the surface of the landscape before him.

Just before splitting up with Calvert, Will had said he might take a wider circle than usual. Calvert did not ask any questions or make any comments. He nodded in his discreet way and rode off on his own. Now as Will surveyed the sweep of land to the west, he calculated how long it would take him to find the homestead west of Popper Spring, ask a few questions, and get back to his pattern. He figured an hour or a little more.

Will checked the cinch on the gray horse, swung aboard, and set off on a lope to the west. Popper Spring would lie a little to the north of where he was riding at the moment. As it was within the area that Calvert would cover, Will held to the west for a good mile and then started angling a few degrees to the north. When he estimated that he had reached a point beyond the spring, he straightened out again and headed west.

The country was not looking any more hospitable. If anything, it looked more austere—the grass dry and brittle, the cactus low and curled, the sagebrush thin and twisted. The soil showed through between the clumps of sparse vegetation, and the ground was littered with rocks—not the smooth, shiny pebbles where water once ran but crusted, mud-colored stones. Will found it curious that a homesteader would want to take up a claim in an area like this.

He rode for another mile until, topping a rise, he saw an unexpected sight. Just ahead lay a protected little valley, surrounded on three sides by ridges, including the one he had just climbed. Down the center ran a thread of water. Will imagined that the valley drifted in with snow during the winter, and the accumulation no doubt helped keep the grass in good condition and helped nourish the cedar trees that grew along the slopes.

Off to his left as the valley ran southward sat a homesteader's cabin and a small set of stock pens. Out from the house, two horses grazed on picket ropes. Farther down the valley to his left, a flock of about eighty sheep grazed. A man with a walking stick moved from the far side of the herd toward the house, and a medium-sized, dark-haired dog trotted beside him.

Will took the gray horse down the slope at a careful walk. By the time the ground leveled out, he was close enough to pick out the unkempt clothes, stained hat, and downer features of Al Stegman. The man stopped, spoke to his dog, and waited for the visitor to cover the rest of the ground between them.

Will rode up to within ten yards of the homesteader and dismounted, so as not to be looming over and talking down to him.

"How do you do? I'm Will Dryden. We met the other day."

Stegman gave a curt nod.

"I was sorry to hear about what happened to Dunn."

"Bein' sorry doesn't do any good."

Will recalled the last time he had been taken to task for saying he was sorry. "I know. But he was a decent man with me, and I thought I'd ride over and see you."

"I don't know what for." Stegman's face had an

empty expression, as if he had no desire for any kind of an exchange.

"Well, for one thing, I understand you gave my name as someone who could vouch for you being friends with Dunn."

Stegman gave a small shrug. "You don't have to admit to it."

"No reason I shouldn't." Will thought the man might have taken some pleasure in letting it be known that one of Donovan's men had been sociable with him and Dunn, but Will didn't see much to be gained by mentioning it. "I just thought that if we were on those terms, it wouldn't be unreasonable for me to drop by."

"Just that, to say hello?"

"I thought that if you didn't mind, you could tell me what things looked like when you found him."

Stegman's face showed a look of true displeasure now. "I found him dead, facedown, out in back of his building."

"Shot?"

"In the back. The bullet went right where the suspenders cross."

"And there were no witnesses?"

Stegman raised his chin and stared at Will with his yellow-brown eyes. "Look, mister. I don't know what you think you stand to gain by puttin' your nose in things."

"Well, I'll tell you. There's a couple of dirty things been done, and I think I've got a hunch who did 'em. But I don't know what the connection is, if there is one, and I figure anything I can find out will help."

"Help do what?"

"Bring things out in the open."

Stegman looked at the ground, tapped once with his walking stick, and raised his head. "I'll tell you what I told the sheriff. I don't know if he's told anyone else, and I don't know how much good it would do for you to repeat it. But that's up to you."

"All right."

"There was a sheepherder claims he saw who did it. He was comin' in over a hill from the north, and he thought he saw somethin' that didn't look right. So he hunkered down, and heard the shot, and then he saw the man ride away."

"And you know this sheepherder from before?"

Stegman gave what Will took for a modest shrug. "I'm a sheepman, so I know some of the others and their herders."

A sheepman. Most of the men Will knew of who called themselves or were called sheepmen had herds into the hundreds or thousands. But that was a small matter. "So how did you happen to talk to him?"

"He stayed hidden out there until I came along. Since he knew me, he came in and told me what he'd seen."

"And then?"

"He went back to his camp, way the hell out on the sheep ranges where his own boss would have a hard time findin' him."

"I see. But you know his name. You gave that to the sheriff?"

"Yes, I did. That's probably the one part I won't repeat to you."

"That's all right. Knowing there's a witness is probably good enough for me for right now."

Stegman's tenseness faded as his shoulders relaxed. "That's about it."

"Maybe one other thing."

"What's that?"

"Did this sheepherder say what the killer looked like?"

"Not to me, but he said he got a look at him."

"That's not much to go on. Do you think he'd recognize him again?"

"I would guess so." After a pause, Stegman added, "Is that it, then?"

"Well, on that part, I suppose so. But if you don't mind, I'd like to talk about something you mentioned the other day."

Stegman slowly shook his head. "I don't know what that would be."

"You said Donovan was pushing you."

"Actually, I think Dunn said that."

"I guess he did, but you added to it. You said you knew what kind of men worked for him and it was time to move on."

Stegman raised his free hand and waved it. "I might have said something like that. It doesn't matter much."

"Oh, don't think I take it personally. Quite the opposite. What I'm interested in is what you know, or have heard, about Donovan's motives for acquiring more land."

"I know he seems to be pretty bent on it."

"Let me put it more directly. Have you heard of this plan he's supposed to be working on, to gather up land for some outside investors?"

"I've heard of it, but I think it's bunk." Stegman sniffed. "I think he's just tryin' to buy up land cheap so he can control big portions."

Will narrowed his gaze. "Do you have an idea what for?"

After a pause, Stegman said, "Accordin' to Dunn, it was for oil. I don't know if he told you any of that."

"He told me about oil, but he didn't tell me that was what Donovan was up to. I sort of put it together, though."

"He was sure Donovan wanted his place, and he said if he came around, he'd tell him to go piss up a rope."

Will smiled. "I can hear him saying that."

"So can I. And judgin' from what happened, it looks as if Dunn was right, though it doesn't do him any good now."

"Sure doesn't." After a few seconds of thought, Will spoke again. "Did Donovan come by here in person?"

"Yes, he did. But not by himself."

"That's what I figured. Did he have his foreman with him?"

"Not Ingram. I know him. He had two others. One of 'em was your friend and mine, Max Aden, and the other was a fellow I didn't recognize."

"Oh, really? What did he look like?"

Stegman shrugged. "Oh, he was a normal-lookin' man, as far as that goes. About your age or a little older. Average size, average build. A hard-looking one, though. He packed a gun, and he had a rifle on his horse, too."

"Any beard or mustache?"

"Not that I remember." Stegman shook his head again.

"Did he say anything?"

"No, Donovan did the talking. He'd already made me an offer before, when I saw him in town. I told him I wasn't interested. Then he sent me a letter and made the offer again. I didn't answer. A month or so later he came by with these other two."

"Did he threaten you?"

"He pretended not to. He told me this wasn't a safe place to live without protection, and he acted as if it was a friendly warning."

"He didn't offer to let you contribute to the protection?"

Stegman shook his head. "Not to me. I heard that was something he did earlier, before I came here."

"So this was a different message."

"Entirely."

"And how long ago was this?"

"Oh, about two weeks—no, maybe a little more. It was just before that kid got killed."

"But you've decided to go?"

"I can see the writing on the wall. I hear he's been goin' around, closin' deals here and there. It's as if he's got a deadline or he's tryin' to beat someone else to it."

"And you've told him?"

"I sent him a letter after I was at Dunn's on Monday."

Will thought for a second. "You don't know if he made an offer to Dunn, though."

"No, I don't, but I know what Dunn would have told him."

"Well, who knows if he got the chance."

Stegman's face had turned hard again. "I'll tell you, it's a dirty way to do things. And I bet it'll be like that kid. No one'll do a damn thing."

"I hope somethin' gets done. Did you know that kid at all?"

The downer face turned down even further. "Yeah,

I knew him. He came by here just like you're doin'. More than once. We talked."

Will narrowed his eyes. "Was he lookin' for someone?" He stopped short of mentioning a name.

"Not exactly. Someone else was, and he was interested."

"Oh, really? How did that go?"

Stegman turned his head, gave his sheep a looking-over, and turned back. "You know, he was sweet on that Indian girl that works in the kitchen."

"I've come to understand that."

"And he didn't trust the way your boss acted around her."

"I wouldn't blame him."

"Then he talked to someone, I don't know who, but it was some man who came around and asked questions about another kitchen girl who disappeared a couple of years ago."

"Before he came here?"

"I believe so. Anyway, he was interested. If your boss had anything to do with this other girl disappearing, then this kid wanted to get the Indian girl out of there before anything happened to her."

"Uh-huh. And who was the man who was looking for this girl who vanished?"

"I don't know. It was someone who worked his way in for a little while and then left. Ben just called him 'the little fella,' and when roundup was done, the little fella went down the road. Said he'd be back in the fall."

"Maybe he will be. If I'm still here, I'll keep an eye out for him."

"Well, I don't intend to be." Stegman hesitated, as

if he had something to say, but he asked, "Is there anything else?"

"One thing. Have you ever heard of a man named Al Vetch?"

Stegman shook his head. "Doesn't sound familiar."

"And Ben Forrester never mentioned the name?"

"Not that I remember."

"I wouldn't think so, but I thought I'd ask."

"Who is he, anyway?"

"I'm not sure, but I've got my hunches. I don't think he's Ben's little fella, though, and I don't think he's the sheepherder at Dunn Station."

"Oh, no. That sheepherder's got a hard name to pronounce."

Will looked down at the dog, which had been sitting in its master's shadow all this time. From there he cast a glance over the sheep, which were all grazing in the same direction, due south.

"Well," he said, "I wish you all the best. I'd better get back to my work."

"Same to you."

Stegman did not release his right hand from his walking stick, so Will saw again that they were not going to shake hands. He turned his horse, set his reins, and mounted up. Without looking back, he took off for his own range.

The gray horse had a smooth trot, so Will let him move at that pace for about a mile and then varied him from a trot to a lope to a walk. As they were going back the way they had just come, Will did not study the land very closely. He let his thoughts wander—now about Dunn, now about Ben Forrester, and now about oil. He wondered where in this empty land a man would drill for oil, and he wondered how a man would know where to try. He reasoned that oil must be like water, and that not every pool had an outlet on the surface.

Will had just loped up a rise, made his horse walk down the gravelly slope on the other side, and was trotting out through the mouth of a dry wash when an object startled him back to the here and now. Right past a low bluff of ancient packed mud, Max Aden sat waiting on the speckled white horse.

The rider was dressed as usual in his large-brimmed hat, neckerchief, denim jacket, chaps, and gun belt. He held his reins in his left gloved hand, which rested overlapping the other on the pommel of his saddle.

As Will reined up and stopped short, Aden called out, "A little ways off your range, aren't you?" The hooked nose and deep-set eyes gave him the look of a hawk.

"No more than you are."

"Always a smart one. What brings you so far this way?"

"I wanted to see what was over the next hill. I'd ask you the same question except that I think I know the answer."

"What would that be?"

"Spyin' on me."

"Bah. You just don't like it when someone sees you wanderin' from your job. You didn't think anyone saw you on Monday, but it came out all the same."

"I wasn't at Dunn Station five minutes, for as much as it's any of your business."

"Fillin' your snoot with whiskey."

"I happened to be buyin' tobacco."

Aden sneered. "Is that right? And what did you run out of today? Mutton?"

Will took the sting. "You'll think mutton. Yes, it so happens I was talkin' to a man who runs sheep. And you might be interested to know about another fella who tends sheep."

"Dyin' to hear." Aden hunched forward and leaned on his gloved hands.

"Seems there was a sheepherder saw who killed Orry Dunn. He's back on his range now, somewhere out north, but when the sheriff asks him, he can give a description."

Aden lifted his head in an arrogant pose. "I don't know why I should care. My presence is spoken for. I was off to the south with Brad Way. As far as that goes, you were a lot closer than that."

"I've got the same alibi you have. Out ridin' with a partner."

"Except that you've got the habit of slippin' off your range, and you're so thick with Jim these days he'd cover for you."

"Oh, go on. I had no quarrel with Dunn, and you know it. And if you doubt my whereabouts, ask Jim. But you won't, because you know he doesn't lie, and you'd rather not know the truth."

"What's that supposed to mean?"

"For one thing, you'd rather just insinuate. And for another, the truth isn't your stock-in-trade."

Aden swung down from his saddle in a second. "Get off your horse, you son of a bitch," he said. He peeled off his jacket, set it across the back of his saddle, then pulled off his gloves and set them on top.

Will stayed seated, and he noticed Aden did not take off his hat or gun belt. That might mean he was trying to goad Will into a gunfight rather than a fist-fight. "What for?" Will asked.

"So I can take you apart."

"Make it easier on yourself. Take off your hat, your chaps, and your gun belt. Then we'll see who walks back to the ranch." After a long moment of waiting, Will shifted his horse to close off Aden's view. When he brought it around again Will had his pistol drawn. "Go ahead, if that's what you had in mind."

The muddy eyes wavered. Aden had his right elbow cocked and his hand hovering above the butt of his pistol. "Piss on you," he seethed. "I get down to fight you man to man, and you pull a gun on me."

"Fight man to man. You had a chance to do that, but you had no intention. That's what I meant about you and the truth. You don't have the stomach to do things fair."

Aden's eyes burned with hatred now. "I knew you were trouble, and I told Earl when he hired you."

"Then tell him to fire me. Tell him where I went and what I heard. Tell him how you tried to pick a fight again. Tell him whatever you want. But don't try to shoot me in the back as I ride away, or you might not get the chance to tell him anything."

"I'd much rather put the bullet through your teeth, so you can see me laughin' at you."

"Wish in one hand," said Will. He put the spurs to the gray horse, and with his pistol still in his hand he loped away. It took all of his self-control not to look back, and he was glad when he came to another rise to go over.

Will found Calvert waiting at their appointed spot. The other man showed no signs of impatience or curiosity as Will dismounted and took a seat near him on the ground. Will took out the makin's for a cigarette, and after a few seconds Calvert asked the usual question.

"See anything?"

"Some sheep."

"Really? Where was that?"

"Over at Stegman's place."

"Oh. Did you get to talk to him?"

"Yes, I did. He's not real talkative to begin with, but he came around a little." Will shook tobacco into the paper trough. "He found Dunn, all right. He also found somethin' else. Accordin' to him, a sheepherder saw who did it. He went back to his range, but the sheriff has his name and ought to be able to get a description from him."

"That should help."

"Dunn had told Stegman about the oil, too, and it seems like that's what Donovan's up to—pretendin' to buy up cheap grazin' land but really tryin' to put together a big tract of land for his own control. Stegman says he's been pushin' here lately to pick up some of the scattered pieces." Will finished rolling the cigarette and licked the seam.

"Who does he think did in Dunn?"

"He didn't say, but he didn't have to."

"And he's selling out, you said before."

Will smoothed the cigarette, stuck it in his mouth, and lit it. "He is. He decided before Dunn got killed, but I'm sure he's even more convinced now. And I don't think it's as much fear as just good sense."

"Well, that's too bad."

"It is. And that's a fair little place he's got."

"If he didn't have sheep."

"I think you have to have it in you to like sheep. I don't."

"Neither do I. But sometimes I don't like cattle,

either, like when they kick you or smear shit all over you."

"Just doin' what they know best." Will took a drag on his cigarette and blew the smoke away on the light breeze. "I heard another interesting thing from this fella Stegman."

Calvert was scratching the inside of the bowl of his pipe with the nail of his little finger. "About sheep?"

"No, not about sheep. About Ben Forrester."

Calvert looked up, serious now. "I guess he knew Ben."

Will nodded. "They got along. And Ben told him something curious. Seems there was a fella here durin' roundup, someone Ben referred to as 'the little fella,' who acted like a hired hand but was lookin' for information."

"I remember a little fella. He went by Bill Parnell, as I recall. Hell, that almost rhymed."

"Almost."

"He wasn't much of a cowpuncher, but if he was here on an operation, I can understand why. Who was he workin' for?"

"I didn't get that. But he was tryin' to find out about a kitchen girl who disappeared a couple of years ago. Does that sound familiar?"

Calvert shook his head. "That would have been before I came here."

"Before Ben, too. He was interested, though, because if something had happened to that girl, then he needed to look out for Pearl. I guess he thought Donovan might have it in him."

"Judgin' from the way things have been goin', I wouldn't put it past him."

"Neither would I. And here's another little thing. I got a chance to talk to Pearl the other evening, for just a couple of minutes, and she said Ben was worried but she didn't know about what. I don't know what else it would be, except what he'd heard."

Calvert tipped his head in thought. "I remember that little fella. He said he'd be back in the fall."

"That's what Stegman said. I figure he either found out as much as he thought he was going to, or he did plan to come back when he could use the cover of bein' a regular hand."

"Could be. He might even learn to rope."

"Anyway, I think it's possible that Ben was onto something and wasn't going to leave it all up to the little fella."

Calvert had a faraway look in his eyes. "I don't remember Ben talkin' all that much to Bill Parnell, but maybe he didn't have to, and if Bill was better at his real work than he was at cowpunchin', he could have had plenty of out-of-the-way conversations." Calvert raised his eyebrows. "I guess you did have an interestin' visit with the homesteader."

"I sure did. Then I had another visit on the way back."

"With the little fella?"

Will laughed. "I have the idea of this little fella bein' like a leprechaun or a dwarf, a skinny little elf that pops up out of the sagebrush. No, I didn't meet him. It was another little man, Max Aden."

"What was he doin'?"

"Spyin' on me, it looked like. And tryin' to pick a fight. I told him where I'd been and what I'd heard about the sheepherder at Dunn's, to let him stew on that."

"What did he say?"

"It didn't seem to faze him. He seemed more in-

terested in makin' a to-do about me wanderin' off
the job. Tried to make it out that I'd slipped over to
Dunn's and shot him. Then he said you and I were
so thick you'd cover for me."

"Ah, he knows better than that. The whole thing."

"That's what I told him. But it seemed to go along
with them not telling us about Dunn to begin with."

Calvert tensed his brows. "In what way?"

"They've got us paired up as not being company
men."

"Oh, they've got to take it a lot farther than that to
make it into something wrong. I do my job, and I
don't lie for anyone. They all know it. And it's no
news to me that I'm not on the inside."

"I didn't take it as a good sign, though."

"To hell with 'em. There's other places to work."
Calvert tapped the bowl of his pipe upside down on
his boot heel. "This thing with Ben, though. It's got
me curious."

"Me, too."

"Who do you think shot him, if everyone on the
ranch was accounted for?"

Will looked straight at his riding partner. "I think
it's someone Donovan keeps out of sight, someone
who's not known around here, and he brings him
out for any crooked work he's got to do."

"Where does he keep him? On the ranch?"

"I think the fella's hidin' out in that little stone
house, and Blanche takes his vittles to him."

Calvert let out a long, low breath. "Right there?"

"I think so. Right under our noses."

"Well, I'll be damned. Do you have any idea who
it is?"

Will looked around at the open country, as if there

might be an eavesdropper within a quarter of a mile, and then he brought his gaze back to Calvert. "I think it's someone Blanche knows, someone Donovan might have found through her. Unless I miss a good bet, I think it's a man called Al Vetch."

Chapter Twelve

Will and his partner saddled fresh horses after the midday meal and rode out of the ranch yard. When they had ridden about half a mile, Calvert turned his horse sideways, checked their back trail, and moved forward again.

"Damnedest thing about that little stone house," he said. "Once you've got the idea that someone's in there, it's not the same."

"I know what you mean. If I hadn't seen Blanche takin' food and water there the other evening, I'd have never had an idea."

"Do you think the old man brought him here just to do a gun job?"

"I think he got him to do some land work. I understand he knows how to work with those kinds of papers. Probably handy at signin' in various hands, too. Then once he was here, someone might have found another job or two for him."

"How much longer do you think he'll stay holed up there?"

"I don't know. I have the idea that most of his work is goin' to be done pretty soon, and he might pull out. So I think we—or I—need to spring something pretty soon, to get him out in the open. My job is just to verify that it's him and report where he is.

After that, it's a matter of whether someone else, like the law, can pin anything on him."

"Just to have things straight—you're not the law, then."

Will laughed. "Not by a long ways. I'm working for a private party, and my job is to locate this fella."

"That's all right. All work is good work."

Will laughed again. "In the meanwhile, if I can get anything else on him, so much the better."

"Such as?"

"I wish there was a way we could talk to this Bill Parnell and ask him about the missing girl that he told Ben about."

"Well, I don't know how to get a hold of him. And I don't know for sure that he'll be back."

By reflex, Will looked behind at the empty landscape. "I'd like to know more about what Ben knew or what he thought he knew."

"That could be hard to find out."

"And Pearl doesn't know much. Not that she could tell me. Just that he was worried there at the end." Will turned to Calvert. "You worked with him. Do you remember noticin' anything?"

"No, I don't, not as far as habits or behavior. You know, I've gone over it a hundred times, and it all seems as normal as daylight. Then last night, when I couldn't sleep, I remembered one little thing."

Will narrowed his attention. "What was that?"

"Funny thing at the time, and you wouldn't think anything about it. Like I've said before, Ben was an easygoin' lad, and every once in a while he'd say somethin' about the Indians—how they tanned their deerskins, how they rode their horses, and the like. Well, he said he wanted to look for arrowheads, and he said he thought he'd go to the old quarry. You know the one."

"Sure."

"Well, Earl Ingram heard him, and he told the kid it wasn't a good place to go—too many snakes—and he'd be better off not goin' there. Ben said he knew how to look out for snakes."

"Did he go, then?"

"I think he planned to on his next day off, but he didn't live long enough."

"That might be somethin'."

"I didn't think anything of it at the time. After all, why would someone kill someone else just to keep him from lookin' for arrowheads? But now that I put it together with this other bit, it seems maybe someone didn't want him to go to the quarry."

"Sounds possible."

"And here's somethin' else I didn't think of. Why would someone look for arrowheads there? With all those chips, it would be like lookin' for a needle in a haystack. Hopeless. And besides, it's the wrong kind of rock."

"Then Ben wasn't very clever, tippin' his hand."

"Doesn't seem like it, but he might have been curious."

"You think he might have expected to find something there, and someone else didn't want him to."

Calvert tapped the loose ends of his reins against his knee. "Doesn't it seem like it, though? After all, who ever spends any time at that quarry? You can see the whole thing from a quarter mile off, and there's never any cattle there. And why run your horse over all those chips?"

"I rode through it, but I was lookin' for a man

whose body I thought might be dumped someplace. I admit I didn't look very close, though. And besides, I was new on the job and didn't want to lose much time or be seen snoopin' around."

Calvert twisted his mouth. "Well, I'm not in the habit of hidin' bodies myself, or of lookin' for 'em, but I'd think that would be a likely place to stash one."

"Sure. And you think that might be what Ben was thinkin'."

"It might be. If Bill Parnell had found somethin' there, the game would be up. But if he told Ben enough to make him want to look on his own, then maybe that's what got him in trouble." Calvert moved his head up and down in slow motion. "It could have been."

The two men rode on for a few minutes until Will spoke. "Are you thinkin' what I'm thinkin'?"

"I don't know. You'll have to tell me."

"It might be interestin' to take a look at that quarry. I barely glanced over it when I went through before."

"That's what I was thinkin', too, except that it won't be in our pattern for a couple of days. And Earl might put us back out diggin' postholes in the meanwhile."

"Well, since I've already got a reputation for wanderin' off my path, I could go over there myself and then tell you what I found."

"Could. But I think it would be safer if the two of us went. And besides, I've got my curiosity up now, too."

Will raised his eyebrows. "Do you want to go over there this afternoon, then?"

"It could be the time to do it. If someone wants to keep an eye on you this afternoon, he can spend a few hours lookin' for you or me either one, out where they think we're headed."

"Shall we go, then?"

Calvert stared ahead. "I say, why not. Up here a ways there's a drainage that'll take us partway across. Then we can skip over a couple of ridges and follow another dry wash." He turned in the saddle and looked back. "Unless someone's followin' us already, it'll be hard to pick us up. I'm glad we've got fresh horses."

With Calvert leading the way, they set off across the dry country. In a little less than an hour of steady riding, they came to the old quarry. At the edge of the rubble, they dismounted and loosened their cinches. The horses had worked up a sweat, and now they could get a little rest even if there was no water.

The site appeared very much as Will remembered it. The rock had been quarried out of the side of a ridge, and the waste had been scattered all along the base. Broken, irregular pieces of stone, ranging in size from a fingernail to a man's head, lay wherever they had landed. Heaps large and small rose from the carpet of rubble. Prickly pear cactus poked through in spots, and here and there Will saw discarded objects such as a rusted can, a bottle, a length of frayed cable, or a scrap of wood.

The quarry was over a hundred yards long, and in some places the trail between the wall and heaps of cast-off rock was barely wide enough to pass on foot. Calvert went first, taking slow steps. He paused and turned.

"You still want to look out for snakes."

"Oh, yeah."

Calvert moved on, and Will followed. Their spurs clinked, and the horse hooves shifted and crunched on the fragments below.

"Looks different up close," said Calvert.

"Sure does. When I came through here before, I followed that trail out there, where it looks like they pulled the wagons."

The wall itself was not a sheer bluff but rather an irregular surface, with crevices and alcoves cutting into it. Will tipped his head back. At its highest point, the wall was fifteen feet or so. Some of the chunks up above looked as if they were ready to let loose and fall, and he imagined several of the pieces on the ground had come down that way. He wiped his brow with the sleeve of his shirt. The rock gave off plenty of warmth.

"This would be a hell of a place to dig a grave," said Calvert. "But if there was a hole, there's plenty of loose rock to cover something up with."

They wandered along, pausing at this cranny or that. Will looked for anything out of place in the overall disorder. On one occasion he thought he saw a mound of rocks that had been placed together. He handed his reins to Calvert and bent to the task of moving the loose pieces. When he got to the bottom, sweat dripping, he found a slab of solid rock. He took his reins back, and the two men ambled on.

Calvert stopped at an opening that was about four feet wide. It ran in for about eight feet, and the back wall tapered upward and outward until it met the bluff about ten feet overhead.

"Here's a place," he said, stepping aside.

Will moved forward and peered in. A layer of loose rock was scattered over the floor of the opening. "Unless it goes down, it's too shallow." Again he handed his reins to his partner. On his hands and knees he crawled in and tossed a few of the top pieces aside. "Nothing here," he said. "Just the slough." He backed out and stood up.

The next place looked more promising. It was a

fissure about two feet wide, running all the way from the ground to the top. As Will craned his neck, he could see over Calvert's shoulder. The gap was about nine or ten feet deep; after a couple of feet in, the opening curved, and beyond the curve lay a mound of rocks about five feet long. Calvert poked his head in, got a better look, and made way for Will.

"Let me try this one." Will handed his reins to Calvert, turned sideways, and stepped in. The crack was a little wider beyond the curve, and he was able to crouch. The air was stale, and the whole crevice lay in the shadow of the rock wall. Will didn't like the feeling of being closed in, but he set to work. Some of the pieces he tossed out behind him, and some he tossed into the open area ahead.

"I wish I had Aden's leather gloves," he said. "This sandstone is rough."

As he moved pieces of rock, he continued to find more loose material below. He sat up straight to catch his breath. If this was a grave, it wasn't very big—probably just large enough for a young woman. He imagined what might lie below—dark hair, a face with unidentifiable features, a dress of gray or light blue fabric.

"Do you want me to spell you?" came Calvert's voice from outside.

"No, I'm all right. It's just that the air's a little close here." Will bent to his work again, kneeled, and resumed pitching the rough pieces.

When he had uncovered about a foot of rock and was working below the ground level he had walked in on, he began to catch a dead smell. He found himself not wanting to see the girl's face, though he knew that after two years it would have a distorted, unreal appearance.

Now his hands moved as if by themselves. His back ached, and he felt as if he was crouched doing his work and watching himself at the same time. He realized he was throwing all the rocks forward. It was easier that way. He cleared them out of the middle first, continuing to pick and toss the pieces that fell in. He stood up to try to clear the haziness, and then he went back to work.

A few minutes later he came to a fabric, a middle tone of blue, neither light nor dark, something like broadcloth. Then the hands—dirty and dented but still with the flesh on them. He was careful not to touch the hands themselves. He moved forward, picking stones off the chest and arms, noting the lapels of the jacket. Farther up, he began to suspend his expectations. He came to the chin and lower face of a man not long dead. The face was twisted and pitted from the weight of the rocks, but it was clearly that of a man who wore a close-trimmed mustache.

Will stood up, stepped back, and took a breath. He needed better air.

Calvert's voice came through the opening. "Did you find something?"

"I sure did." He sidestepped back from the interior and out into the daylight. Taking a couple of deep breaths of air, he fought down the heaving urge to vomit. "Take a look for yourself," he said, "but don't breathe too deep."

In less than a minute, Calvert came out of the opening and expelled his breath. "It's Bill Parnell," he said. "I guess he wasn't as good at his work as he should have been."

"Doesn't seem like it."

"Where do you think the girl is?"

"I would say he was looking for her out here and didn't find her. But they found him."

Calvert had a thoughtful look on his face as he nodded. "He let everyone think he was gone, and then he came back. No one was goin' to miss him."

"Too bad. I'd say he thought the girl was out here, and Ben thought so, too. They didn't want Ben comin' here to the quarry because if he did, he'd find this fella."

"Whew." Calvert let out a long breath. "What about the girl, then?"

"We can look around here some more, but chances are, she's somewhere else, if at all."

"You think this might have all been a false lead?"

Will shook his head. "I don't think so, but we can't assume anything. If this fella made one mistake, he could have made two."

Calvert looked at the ground with his eyes wide open. "He sure helped Ben make one as well, then."

"We all make mistakes. You and I just have to make sure we don't make any big ones now."

They searched the rest of the quarry without finding anything. As they led their horses away from the field of rubble, Will looked up at the sky. The sun had moved over but was not yet slipping in the west.

"Here's an idea," he said as he checked his rigging and tightened his cinch. "One of us can go to town, and the other can go back to the ranch at the usual time."

"What do we need in town?"

"The sheriff, for one thing, and the person I'm workin' for, for another. I'd like to show her Al Vetch, and then the sheriff can hold him if he thinks he has enough cause. At the very least, he needs to know about Bill Parnell."

Calvert, still calm, said, "I'd guess you want to go to town."

"Actually, I think it would look better if you did. Raise less suspicion at the ranch."

"But this person you're workin' for—you said it was a she—don't you think you should be the one to talk to her?"

"I can do that when she gets to the ranch. I'd like to keep an eye on things, to the extent that I can."

"What if she doesn't take my word for it?"

"I can write her a note."

"What do you plan to tell the others?"

"I don't know. I'm still tryin' to think this through. What's a good idea?"

Calvert looked up at his hat brim. "Let's see. You can tell 'em I cut my hand open when I was tryin' to take a cactus out of a calf's lip. I saw a fella do it one time, so I know it can be done."

"That sounds like it'll work. Now how about if you lend me your tally book and pencil, and I'll write the letter."

Calvert reached into his saddlebag and brought out the booklet and pencil. "Here." Then he pulled out his gun and holster. "Might as well put this on while I'm at it."

Will flipped past the first couple of pages, which had writing on them, and found a blank one. On it he wrote his message.

Mrs. Welles:

I believe I have found what I have been looking for. Please come with Jim Calvert to the Redstone

Ranch. He is a trustworthy man I have mentioned before and he will drive you.

Respectfully,
Will Dryden

He showed the note to Calvert, who asked, "When do you expect us to be there?"

"Tomorrow morning would be good. I think it would be too much of a rush to try to get there this evening, and something could go wrong in the dark."

"Same with the sheriff?"

"If you can get him."

"Good enough." Calvert tucked the tally book into his vest pocket. "Maybe one other thing."

"What's that?"

"Where do I find this woman?"

"Oh. That would help. Ask for Irma Welles at the Continental Hotel. She's supposed to be staying there for a few more days."

"And I'm to hire something to drive her out in?"

"Um, yes. I think she'll pay for it. If not, I'll pay you later. I don't have any money on me right now."

Calvert held up his hand. "Don't worry. I'll take care of it one way or the other."

"All right. Best of luck."

"Same to you. Let's get the hell away from this place."

With one look behind at the quarry, Will swung onto his horse and put it into a lope. He and Calvert rode together until they came to a set of breaks. Calvert signaled that he would go to the right while Will would go to the left. Raising his hand and giving a tip of the head, Jim Calvert headed for town. Will kept on to the northwest, and when he came to the head of the draw he rode up on top. Shading his eyes with his hand at the edge of his hat brim, he scanned the country. It looked as empty as always, and he knew that was an illusion.

Earl Ingram listened to the story with attention as the men waited in the bunkhouse for the supper bell. "I thought Jim was more careful than that," he said, fixing his eyes on Will.

"I think it could happen to anyone once." Will sat down in the chair by the square table, about eight feet from where Ingram sat. He did not want to give the foreman the impression that he was avoiding him.

"Why didn't he come back here? We've got everything for that—iodine, bandages."

"He seemed pretty worried. He wanted to see if he could get a doctor to sew it up."

Ingram shifted the toothpick in his mouth. "Laid it open pretty good, then."

"Right between the heel and the palm." Will drew his finger along the thickest part of his left hand.

"Where did it happen?"

"About a mile south of Popper Spring."

"What time was it?"

"Midafternoon when he found me. About three o'clock."

Ingram's blue eyes had been roving, and now they settled to meet Will's. "And what did you do after that?"

"Rode my circle as usual."

"Then some of Jim's didn't get covered."

"That's right. If you want, I can ride that part in the morning." Will cut the deck on the table in front of him and looked at the five of clubs.

"We'll see about it then." Ingram seemed to reconsider something. "When do you think he'll be back?"

"I wouldn't be surprised if he showed up tomorrow morning."

"He's staying overnight in town, then."

"I believe that's what he intended."

Ingram pushed out his mustache. "I should send Max in to make sure he's all right."

Will looked over at Aden, who lay in his bunk with his arms across his chest. "Oh, then Brad and I can work together tomorrow."

The foreman did not seem to like the idea. "We'll see about that in the morning."

A few minutes later, Blanche sounded the triangle. The men rose to their feet, and Will waited to be the last out the door. With Calvert gone, he felt the whole group was out of balance.

Donovan showed up for supper with his gray hair well combed and with his white-handled revolver hanging on his belt. He listened to Ingram, who spoke in a low tone of voice that was nevertheless audible to everyone at the table as well as to Blanche, who cocked an eyebrow as she delivered the fried ham.

Donovan nodded at the empty seat across from him and said to Will, "Earl says Jim had an accident."

"Yes, sir, he did. Cut his hand."

"Left you to work by yourself."

"Yes, but I don't mind it. We're on our own most of the time as it is."

"Oh, it's good to have someone to look out for you, though. Just like Jim had you. That's why Earl has you men work in pairs. Isn't that right, Earl?"

Ingram nodded. "You bet. But even that's no guarantee. Had a fellow one time, he was skinnin' a steer on the ground, and you know how some people pull the knife towards 'em. Well, he did it, and it must have slipped, because he got himself right here on the inside of his thigh. Bled to death before anyone knew it, and him just on the other side of the chuck wagon."

"Always work the knife away from you," said Donovan. "That's what they taught us."

"Can never be too careful," Ingram continued. "I'm surprised at Jim, though. He's as careful as any man I know."

"Which of these boys does the whittlin'?" Donovan asked.

Ingram pointed as he answered. "Brad does."

"Then you know to always work your knife away from you, don't you?"

"Yes, sir."

"That's good. Try not to have any accidents on the ranch."

Will sat inside the open barn door and kept a watch on the other buildings. After a while, Blanche came to the door of the cookshack, stood there for a moment, and stepped out into the night. Again she was carrying a pail and a jug, and she headed in the direction of the little stone house. Will chose not to follow her, as he did not want to upset anyone's sense of ease at this point. For the same reason, he decided not to go into the kitchen and seek a conversation with Pearl. He waited until Blanche's form was absorbed into the darkness and he heard the scrape of a door. Then, noting that one room was lit in the ranch house, he crossed the yard in the dark.

Leaning against the hitching rail closest to the cookshack, he rolled a cigarette and lit it. The front door of the bunkhouse was closed, probably because Jim Calvert was not there to leave it open as he smoked his pipe. Blanche had left the door of the cookshack open, however, and Will kept a casual gaze in that direction.

After a couple of minutes, Pearl appeared in the doorway. She stood with her left hand on the doorjamb as she peered out.

Will cleared his throat and stood up straight. The action caught her attention, and she motioned for him to come near.

"Evenin'," he said in a low voice as he came within a few feet and into the light.

"Good evening," she answered. "I need to ask you something."

"Go ahead."

"Is Jim all right?"

"Sure he is. Are you worried about him?"

"Just a little. He didn't get hurt some other way, did he?"

"Oh, no. He's all right. He's just spendin' the night in town."

She gave a sigh of relief. "You never know. Someone gets hurt bad, and everyone else acts like nothing happened."

"I know what you mean, but don't worry. I expect him to be back out here tomorrow before noon."

"Well, thank you."

"Don't mention it."

A sound carried across the night, the sound of wood scuffing. Will stepped back from the light of the doorway. He looked in the direction of the little stone house but saw nothing. When he brought his glance back to the doorway of the cookshack, Pearl had vanished. He cupped his lit cigarette and held it in front of him as he turned and walked to the far end of the bunkhouse. Once there, he stepped around the corner.

As he smoked his cigarette in the darkness, he mulled over the situation. He was sure Ingram was suspicious, but that was to be expected from people who had something to hide. Jim Calvert, at least, should be in a safe place by now. Will smiled at the thought of Jim having a drink with Mrs. Welles, though he was pretty sure Jim would be careful not to make any mistakes.

Then he thought of another man off in a different direction, a little fella lying on his back, partially covered with loose rock. It was too bad for the dead man, but it would give the sheriff something to go on. It would also give Bill Parnell the chance for a decent burial. Every man—or woman—deserved that.

Chapter Thirteen

In the lantern light of the cookshack, Earl Ingram pushed aside his breakfast plate and took out his watch to wind it. He leveled his calm blue eyes on Will and said, "Go ahead and cover that ground that Jim didn't get to. If he's back by noon, then the two of you can go on ahead as you would have done." Ingram turned to his right. "Max, you and Brad can work to the southeast."

Will finished his coffee, put his plate and cup and fork in the wreck pan, and stepped outside into the cool morning. He went to the horse corral, roped out the sorrel he intended to ride, and led him to the hitching rail.

A few minutes later, Brad Way came out of the cookshack, took a final drag on his cigarette, and stepped on the butt. Will imagined Aden still sitting inside in a haze of smoke and conferring with Ingram. From Will's estimate, Aden must have ridden quite a ways across country to check on him yesterday, and he might be getting the go-ahead to do the same thing today.

Will was pulling the rear cinch when Aden came out at a brisk walk, the tip of his cigarette glowing in the gray light. He coughed once and kept heading for the barn. As Will mounted up to ride out of the ranch yard, he saw Aden going into the horse corral with his rope.

A light shone through the cookshack window, but Will did not see anyone within as he rode past. Ingram was probably still sitting at the table, taking his time with a cup of coffee. Will glanced around at the two stone buildings, one small and one large, both of them gray in the morning twilight. All the windows were dark, and the two buildings sat silent as headstones.

With a clucking sound, Will put the sorrel into a trot. He held that pace for nearly a mile, and then he turned on the trail to survey the country behind him. The sky was turning shades of yellow and pink in the east, but the grassland itself still had the predominant cast of gray. It looked as if the day was starting out like any other, but if things went anywhere near the way he hoped, he was going to turn over a pretty big applecart. This was probably his last day at the Redstone, so he wasn't too worried about starting it off by not going where he was expected to be.

He had it in mind that instead of riding the circle he should be at the ranch when Jim Calvert showed up, and if Aden was busy trying to find him out on the range, so much the better. Meanwhile, he wanted to keep an eye on the buildings. Following a route that kept to low ground, he headed east and came out on a rise just north of the Redstone headquarters.

Far off to the south he saw two riders, which would be Aden and Brad Way starting out on their rounds. Closer in, he saw the horse pasture dotted with grazing animals, then the corrals and barn and other buildings. Sunrise was casting light over the scene, which was still and quiet. Smoke rose from the stovepipe on the cookshack, and horses moved in the corral, but no humans appeared.

Then he had a small surprise. Earl Ingram came out of the cookshack, crossed to the barn, and fetched a horse from the corral. A few minutes later, he rode off in the direction Will had taken earlier.

As stillness returned to the ranch yard, Will decided this could be the time to make his move. Mounting up, he rode farther east and then came around, making his approach so that the bunkhouse stayed between him and the yard. Once he got to the bunkhouse, he dismounted and walked along the wall to the corner. He peeked around and saw no one. He took a couple of steady breaths to calm himself and then stepped into the open, leading the horse. He crossed the yard to the barn without looking to either side, but once there, he glanced out and saw that the cookshack door was closed. If anyone had seen him, it would be Donovan, but Will had gotten the idea that the boss slept late.

Now for the cover. Will tied the sorrel to a post and went to the workbench where the horseshoeing tools were kept. He found a pair of long-handled nippers and returned to the horse. Lifting the right rear foot and holding it in his lap as he crouched, he used the nippers to wrench the horseshoe loose. Now, if anyone asked him what he was doing, he could say his horse was losing a shoe and he had come back to try to fix it.

Next he took off his spurs, put them in his saddlebag, and pulled a bundle of burlap bags close to the doorway. He sat there and waited for over an hour, rolled a cigarette and lit it, and went back to look through the stable and corrals. Still seeing nothing, he took a seat by the open door again and resumed his watch.

He had lapsed into absentminded staring when all of a sudden the cookshack door opened and his pulse jumped. Blanche stepped outside into the bright sunlight, and without looking around she set off carrying a pail and a jug.

About a minute later, Pearl appeared at the doorway, shading her eyes against the morning sun.

Will gave a low whistle, and her eyes searched him out. He made the sound again and stepped more fully into view, but he stayed inside the open doorway of the barn.

She gave a frowning, inquiring look, and he waved for her to come his way. She frowned again, and he repeated his gesture. She looked both ways, and then, holding the lower part of her apron on each side to the fabric of her brown dress, she stepped into full view and crossed the yard.

"What do you want?" she whispered, once she was inside the doorway.

"How long is Blanche going to be gone?"

"I don't know. Sometimes at this time of day she stays there for a little while." Her dark eyes roved over him. "What is it?"

"I'd like to know some things if I can."

"Like what?"

"Along the lines of what we were talking about the other night before Blanche came along."

She turned to glance out at the empty yard. "I don't know what else there is."

"We were talking about Ben." He paused, trying not to jump into the topic too fast. "You said he was worried. Was it about something he knew or about something he thought might happen?"

It took her a few seconds to answer. "Maybe a little of both."

"Was he worried for you, or for himself, or—"

"Again, probably some of both." Her eyes seemed to be searching him. "He said he wanted to get me out of here before anyone got hurt, but he didn't make it."

"Is that something you'd like to do?"

"Get out?"

"Yes."

She hesitated, as if she was uncertain about being so direct with him. Then she spoke in a calm voice. "Yes, I would. I wish I could get away from here, but I don't know how I can. Blanche keeps such a close eye on me, and Frank tells me he'd hate to see me ever leave. I don't see how I could just walk out of here."

"I told you the other evening I would help you if I could, and I'll try to make good on that. I think things are going to change pretty soon, and the more I know, the better chance I'll have of helping you get out of here."

She looked at him as if she didn't know how much to believe. "What else is there to know?"

"Maybe a few things. Did Ben ever mention a girl who worked in the kitchen before you did?"

"He asked me if I had heard of her."

"Had you?"

"Yes, but not much."

Will felt his heartbeat pick up. "What all did you hear? Did you know her name?"

"Yes, I heard her name. Blanche called me by it a couple of times by mistake when I first came. Her name was Marie."

"Marie. Do you know what her last name was?"

"No. Just Marie." Pearl looked over her shoulder. "I should be going."

"Wait another minute if you can. I've got a couple of other things I'd like to ask about."

"Well, hurry."

"Okay. First, do you remember a man who worked here a while back, named Bill Parnell? A little fella."

She nodded. "I remember him."

"Did Ben say anything about him?"

She gave a thoughtful expression and shook her head. "Not that I remember. Why?"

"Well, he might have been looking for this girl Marie, or what happened to her, and he might have said something to Ben. It could have been part of what Ben was worried about. I doubt that anyone has said anything about Bill Parnell since he left."

She shook her head. "No."

"And I doubt that they ever talk about Marie."

"No, not that, either."

Will took a deep breath and exhaled. "Tell me this if you can, Pearl. Do you know who's hiding out in the little stone house?"

She held her eyes steady as she said, "No."

"But it's someone Blanche knows, and someone you're not supposed to make a peep about."

Her eyes wavered and came back to him. "That's right."

Will thought he heard a sound in the stable, but before he checked to see, he said, "Just one more thing, quick. Have you ever heard of a man called Al Vetch?"

A voice came from behind him, a rough voice he recognized. "Hold it right there, puncher. I can shoot either of you or both, and don't think I'm afraid to shoot the girl."

He turned around to see Blanche standing on the other side of the sorrel horse with both hands together on the seat of the saddle. She held a dark pistol, a .38 from the looks of it, with the hammer back.

"Stand over there," she said, "and don't think of touching your gun." She came around the hindquarters of the horse and kept the pistol trained on Will. "And you, dearie," she said to Pearl, "stand over here on my left. Don't try anything foolish, or your friend the snoop gets a hole in him."

Will found his voice. "You might want to be careful about what you do here. The sheriff's on his way."

Her face turned down in an expression of contempt. "You shit and fall back in it. I suppose the governor's comin' with him."

"Don't believe me if you don't want to, but where do you think Jim Calvert went?"

Blanche hesitated and glanced at the doorway. Will held still and tried to keep his eyes off Pearl, who was moving around to Blanche's left.

Will spoke again. "Make it easy on yourself."

"Easy? Nothin's easy. Especially for you, Mr. Snoop." Then Blanche's face fell and she turned her head ever so slightly to the left. Pearl held a small pistol against the front of Blanche's ear, below the temple.

"Let him have the gun," Pearl said. "Just remember what you said about me a minute ago."

Pearl's hand holding the pistol followed Blanche's head as the older woman turned and relaxed the gun in her hand. Will stepped forward, took the revolver, and eased the hammer down.

"Thanks, Pearl," he said. "I think Blanche will cooperate now."

As the young woman lowered her pistol, Will

caught a view of it. It was a small, black-handled .32, the kind that some men used for a hideout gun in a boot or pocket.

"Where did you get that?" he asked.

"Ben gave it to me."

"Good. I think you'd better hang on to it. Now I suggest you go back to the kitchen and stay there until things are over." He tried to guess what time it was. Maybe nine o'clock, maybe later. He wondered what was taking Jim Calvert so long, and he wondered how soon Earl Ingram would be back. The fat was in the fire now, though, and he couldn't sit around and wait.

Holding Blanche's .38 pointed toward the floor, he spun the cylinder and saw all six chambers were loaded. He poked out one cartridge, let the hammer down on the empty cylinder, and slipped the loose cartridge into his pants pocket. Then he shifted the .38 to his left hand and tucked it into his belt as his right hand rested on the handle of his .45.

"You and I can go now, Blanche."

She gave him a sour look. "Where?"

"I want you to take me to Al Vetch."

"Sure," she said, though her voice had a quaver to it. "He'll know what to do with the likes of you."

"Let's go, then. Pearl, as soon as we get started, you can go across to the kitchen."

With that, he took hold of Blanche's upper arm, and the two of them stepped out into the daylight and started walking toward the stone house. At the edge of his vision he saw Pearl cross the yard and go into the cookshack.

Blanche, meanwhile, had not run out of steam. "You think you're smart, mister, forcin' me to take you there. But I'll tell you, it's a good way to get hurt."

"I'm not forcin' you. I'm just holdin' on so you don't get there too far ahead of me. If you'd rather, we can go sit in the kitchen till the sheriff gets here. Either way, no one has to get hurt."

They marched up to the solid wood door that was on the right side of the little house. Blanche gave it a couple of raps.

"It's me," she said.

Will heard the scrape of a chair, followed by the turning of a latch, and the door opened halfway. A gravelly voice said, "I didn't expect you back so soon, Puss."

Will guessed the man was standing to one side of the doorway, as he himself was, and could see only the woman. She had a petulant look on her face, and her voice had an irritated tone as she spoke out.

"Al, he's right behind—"

Will crossed in back of her, turning her to face the opening, and with his left shoulder he pushed the door inward, out of the man's hand. Then he pushed Blanche into the room, released her, and got the drop on Al Vetch.

"Hold it there," he said, before taking a full view of the man. The first thing he looked for was a gun, and he was glad to see that the man did not have one in either hand and was not even wearing his gun belt. Then he saw something that almost made him dizzy.

As he focused on the man's features, he felt a prickly sensation, a crawling chill, up the center of his back and neck and through his scalp. It was the chill he would expect if he had opened a lady's hatbox and had seen the head of a snake rise out of it. The man was not wearing a hat, and his hair was ridged down to give his head the appearance of a bullet. That unfamiliar feature aside, Will recognized the hard, thickening face and the eyes full of contempt. It was the man from the card game in Enfield, the man who had taken a dislike to him and had caused him to be thrown in jail. Will felt as if he suddenly had much more on his hands than he had bargained for.

"Who the hell are you?" asked the man. "And what are you doin' bargin' in here like this?" His eyes wandered, no doubt looking for an opportunity to change the layout.

"I'm Will Dryden. I would think you would remember seein' me once or twice."

"When was the first time?"

Will kept his eyes roving from the man's eyes to his hands and back to his eyes. "In Enfield. Less than a month ago."

The brows raised in an expression of casual disregard. "I don't remember you."

"Maybe it doesn't matter."

"When was the second time?"

"Last Sunday, on the edge of town near the livery stable."

"Oh, was that you? I should have put a bullet through you."

"Why didn't you?"

"It wasn't the plan." Vetch narrowed his eyes. "Oh, yeah. I remember you. In the card game." He turned his head a quarter turn and gave a sarcastic smile. "Is that why you came here?"

"Yeah. I wanted to know why you beat me up."

"Because I didn't like you, that's why. If I'd known you were the same guy the other night, I would have laughed at you."

"It's not too late."

"Of course it isn't." He turned to Blanche and held his hands out to each side. "Can you believe this? He's the same chump that—"

"Get around straight and hold your hands where I can see them."

Vetch frowned and gave a dark, sideways look. "Don't come in and boss me around, or I'll make you the cabin boy." He took a step toward Blanche. "Don't you think he'd make a good—"

"Turn around!"

"Oh, go tell someone who'll listen."

Vetch waved his left hand, then dove in front of Blanche, whose figure blocked Will's vision for a second. Vetch came up on the other side of her with a six-gun in his hand. The dark eyes searched for a spot to place his shot, but Will had taken two steps aside and was bringing up his gun. Vetch whirled, swung his left hand to push Blanche out of the way, and was bringing his gun around when Will shot him in the chest. Vetch's gun waved and jerked, and a shot splintered the door. Will held the gun on the man where he had landed and now sat on the floor. Vetch had it in him to fight till the end. Although his eyes held a vacant, faraway expression, he raised the gun and had his finger on the trigger. Will shot him off-center between the chest and the shoulder, and as he fell backward his gun clattered on the floor.

Will stood back, waiting to be sure Al Vetch did not move again. At that moment Blanche rose from the cot where she had been thrown, and screaming for help, she bolted through the open door. Will raised his gun but did not see any point in stopping her that way, so he let her go.

With a backward glance at the body on the floor, Will moved to the edge of the doorway and peered out. Blanche had taken off like a runaway horse and was more than halfway to the cookshack, screaming as she ran.

Now things were a mess, way out of his control, as if he had tossed his rope at a calf and had caught a grizzly. He didn't know when Calvert was coming back, and he knew that if he stepped out of the little house, Donovan or one of the others could fill him with lead. If he didn't get out, they could come and get him.

He gazed at the dead man on the floor. So this was what it came to. He liked to think that this was the consequence of a certain way of life, but he knew better. If it happened to Ben Forrester, it could happen to him, Will Dryden, just as well as to Al Vetch.

Chapter Fourteen

As Will put two new cartridges into the cylinder of his six-gun, he took stock of Vetch's hideout. The stone house was a one-room building, sparsely furnished. Against the back wall lay the cot with a rumpled gray blanket. About a yard out from the left wall, a chair stood behind a table, while the table itself was littered with dirty plates and bowls. A lard pail and a gallon jug sat on the floor below the table. Against the right wall, two wooden crates, one on top of another, served as a rack for the man's saddle. A bridle was slung on the pommel, and the butt of a rifle stuck out of a scabbard.

Will figured he could use the rifle if necessary, just as he could use Vetch's pistol or Blanche's. He didn't like that line of thought, though. If it came to being pinned down in here, all the ammunition in the room might give him twenty minutes.

He found Vetch's gun belt on the floor. He imagined it had been on the end of the cot when Vetch made a dive for it. Seeing that the dead man's cartridges were .45's just like his, he took out all fifteen and put them in his left pants pocket. He preferred to leave the pistol on the floor where it had fallen.

Next he went to the saddle and pulled the rifle partway out of the scabbard. It was a bolt-action

Spencer, which he didn't care for, so he slipped it back into its boot.

He rested his hand on the grip of Blanche's pistol, and as he reviewed things in his mind, he remembered he had a .38 cartridge in with all the .45's. Just another minute, he thought, to keep from making a mistake. He reached deep into his pocket and dug out a handful of shells, and he found the shiny .38 with the dark bullet. He plucked it out, put it in his right pocket, and poured the .45's back into his left.

He looked out the door again. Nothing stirred. He felt as if he had been in this room way too long. Donovan could be hiding inside his front door with a rifle, or one of the others could have come back by now. He didn't like being in a room with only one door. They could come right in and get him if they had the nerve.

He surveyed the empty ranch yard again. The best place to be, he figured, was the cookshack. It had a front door and a back one, and it commanded a good view. He also needed to find out whether Blanche or Pearl had the upper hand. If Blanche had gotten the little pistol from Pearl, the trouble could start all over again.

He set his plan. He would zigzag across the hard-packed yard, in full daylight, and hope no one could draw down on him well enough as he moved. One more look. He pulled out the .38 from his belt so that it wouldn't jab him and he would have a gun in his hand. Ready. And he made a break for it.

Running in a crouch with the pistol in his right hand, he expected at every step to feel a bullet slam into him. Every few steps he lifted his head to be sure he was still on course. Finally he reached the cookshack, with no sounds all the way except his own labored footfalls and breathing.

The door opened as he turned the knob and pushed, and he came to a stop right inside. A man sat at the mess table facing the door, a man with his hat removed and his hair pressed down. At first Will thought it was Al Vetch again, but as his eyes adjusted to the unlit interior, he saw that it was Earl Ingram. The man had his hands together on the table, and he smiled as he spoke in a calm, smooth voice.

"Well, hello, Will. You're back early, aren't you?"

Will held the .38 level but not pointed right at the foreman. "So are you."

"I never left. I've been waiting all this time for you. I knew you didn't want to work by yourself today, and I figured you would come back."

"Where's Blanche?"

Ingram tipped his head toward the kitchen. "She's in there, makin' biscuits."

Will listened but heard nothing at all. "Where's Pearl?"

"Why, she's helping measure the flour." Ingram smiled again. "What's the matter, Will? Are you worried about that girl? Or do you want her for yourself?"

"You know what's up."

Ingram slowly shook his head. "No, I don't. You'll have to tell me."

"Maybe you could tell me."

"About what?" Ingram raised his eyebrows in an expression of innocence.

"About Marie."

"Marie was my little sister. She died of the whooping cough when she was ten. I don't know why you want to mention her."

"Or Bill Parnell. What was he, your little brother?"

"Well, I think someone has been tellin' you things

and has got you worked up. Listenin' to someone like Stegman could get you in trouble."

"I got it from Bill Parnell himself."

Ingram's mouth and mustache made a circle. "Oh? Did you?"

"Yes, I did. Yesterday."

"I see. Was he having a cup of tea with your home-steader friend?"

From Ingram's breezy tone, Will could tell the foreman thought he was bluffing. "No," said Will. "I found him out at the quarry, lying on his back."

Ingram's face stiffened, but he kept up his own game. "No one wants to work anymore. Look at you—and Jim, for all I know."

Will did not answer the comment about Jim. Rather, he was watching Ingram's shoulders, which had started to twitch as if the man was getting ready to make a move.

"Stand up," said Will, pointing the gun right at him.

"What do you mean?"

"I mean stand up, and keep your hands together in front of you."

"What for?"

"So I can take your gun and hold you as a murder suspect until the sheriff gets here."

Ingram gave a forced laugh. "We all joke a lot, don't we? A newcomer wouldn't know when we were seri-ous and when we weren't."

Will thumbed back the hammer on the .38. "I mean it. Stand up. I think you know where I just came from, and we're all done jokin'."

Ingram held his hands at waist level but not quite together as he rose from his seat. The gun belt and dark-handled six-shooter came into view. He seemed to waver in his balance, and rather than step over the bench, he edged backward against it. The bench hit the floor with a knock and a thump, which made Will flinch.

At that moment, Ingram pointed at the kitchen and hollered, "Look out!"

By reflex, Will jerked his gun toward the kitchen doorway, and seeing nothing, he came back around to Ingram.

The man had drawn his six-gun and had brought it up so that Will could see the open end of the muzzle.

Will pulled the trigger, and a red spot appeared on Ingram's clean gray shirt. The foreman lifted his .45 and lowered it, trying to steady his aim, and Will put a bullet through the brown wool vest. The man fell back and to his right, and the bench rattled as he hit the floor.

Will shifted the .38 to his left hand, wondering whether to put the remaining shell in it or not to bother with the gun at all. Taking soft steps to the kitchen, he peeked in to make sure no one was there. After a quick search he found the flour bin and pulled it open. It was about three-quarters full. With the wooden scoop he made a temporary grave for the .38 and covered it over.

At the doorway to the eating area he paused, craning his neck. Ingram lay with his arm outstretched and his gun a yard away. He was a tight one to the last card, all right. Will wondered how long he had been sitting here—he could have come in through either door while Pearl was talking in the barn or while Will was in the stone house. Will's glance fell on Ingram's hat, which lay brim down on the table. On a hunch, he walked over and lifted the hat. There lay the little .32, which gave Will an idea of whether Pearl still had the upper hand.

He pondered what to do with the pistol. At first he thought of covering it with the hat again, but he didn't like the idea of it falling into the wrong hands. He set the hat aside and lifted the .32 with his left hand. He carried it to the kitchen, where he found an open burlap sack of beans. With a shove he buried the gun, then smoothed the dry beans over the surface.

At the doorway again, with his hand on the grip of his .45, he paused to think about what he needed to do next. He assumed Blanche had strong-armed Pearl, and he imagined they had gone to the ranch house, but he wasn't sure of the best way to approach it.

As he stood pondering, staring at Ingram's hat on the table, the back door of the cookshack burst open, and Max Aden jumped in with his gun drawn. When he landed he hopped to the right, then swept the room with his deep-set eyes and his pistol moving together. He looked as fierce and intent as a hawk. It was evident that he was having to let his vision adjust after being out in the bright daylight, and he probably did not expect to find his man at the kitchen doorway. When he came around that far he gave a wider target than before, but still not a big one.

Will had his .45 in position and shot once, twice, three times. Aden's left shoulder jerked back, but he still held his gun up and fired. The shot whistled through the doorway to Will's right and pinged through a pot on the kitchen wall. Before the man could shoot again, Will bore down and put a shot dead center below the loose red neckerchief. Aden snapped back, and his large-brimmed hat fell in the doorway and rolled outside.

Keeping the man covered, Will stepped around the end of the long table. Aden lay about five feet from Ingram, the two of them more similar than Will had ever seen them in life. One difference was that instead of a mustache, Aden had a seam of blood between his lips.

Will let out a long breath, and with his hands trembling from the rush of action, he poked out the four empty casings and replaced them with good cartridges. His mouth was dry, and the pit of his stomach was pounding. He took a few more deep breaths to steady himself.

He tried to place things in relation to one another. Donovan was no doubt holding out in the ranch house. He would have heard shots, and he would take warning. Will could picture him sitting in an armchair with a rifle across his knees, the grandfatherly smile all gone, replaced by a look of stale displeasure.

As for Jim Calvert, Will hoped he was rolling across the plain, and none too slow. If he was still lingering in town, or if he had been unable to find the sheriff, things could drag on all day.

Meanwhile, there was the matter of Blanche and Pearl. Will had no idea where they were or whether Blanche had gotten hold of another firearm.

Time was wasting, and he needed to start his search. Stepping around the bodies, he went out through the doorway into the bright sunlight. As a practical matter he checked both outhouses, then made as little noise as possible as he approached the back door of the bunkhouse. He could not imagine who could be inside, but even a frightened Brad Way could pose a danger. After a second's thought, Will gave three sharp raps on the door, then three more. Quick as he could, he ran around to the front door and, gun in hand, burst in.

The place was empty, deathly still after the last two buildings he had gone into. The bunks, all silent in the dim light, looked like two rows of graves in a cemetery. Ben Forrester's personal items, including his black hat, still sat on the cot that had become his after his death. Ingram's and Aden's now joined that company.

Will kept his gun in hand as he walked the length of the bunkhouse and back. Nothing moved, but one thing struck him as curious. Aden's chaps hung on the wall by his bunk. Maybe he had expected to have a gunfight today and didn't want anything to hamper his movement. Will shook his head. It didn't matter much now.

The sight of Jim Calvert's bunk brought him back to the moment. Time was still ticking, even if he couldn't hear it. He went out the back door and into the daylight again.

At the space between the two buildings, he moved to the front and looked out at the yard. A tiny whirlwind skipped along, raising dust and small particles of dried grass. As soon as it passed, everything was as motionless as before. He turned his head to study each detail again—the barn, the stable, the corrals, the little stone house, the larger one to its right. Then a sound broke the silence.

He heard the crash of breaking glass, then the high, piercing scream of a woman. It was not Blanche's scream, he knew that, and the pitch of it sent a flood of alarm through his whole body.

Something in the scream told him that Donovan had his hands on the girl, and if he did, he was not waiting at the door with a rifle. He might have his white-handled sidearm for closer work, but that was not going to keep Will out of the house.

He ran full bore past the cookshack, past the open spot on his right where he half expected to see a stranger, up the worn path between the two patches of dry weeds, and up the stone steps of the ranch house. The front door stood ajar, and he paused at the threshold as he drew his gun.

Commotion sounded from within, like someone dragging or shoving another person up or down a staircase, but because of the position of the door, Will could not place the sound. He pushed the door with his foot, and it swung open without a squeak.

He stepped inside onto a wood floor that at one time had carried a good finish. Now the surface was worn and scratched, with the route of most wear leading past a front room on the right and down a hallway. He followed the path and came to a dark, unoccupied kitchen and dining room on the left and a stairway on the right leading up and back toward the front of the house.

He rounded the foot of the staircase and headed up. Keeping to the right or open side, he took the steps two at a time. He tried to make as little noise as possible, but he knew it was pointless to try to be silent. Donovan knew things had broken loose, and no one was going to walk in on him with his back turned.

The upstairs consisted of four rooms—two vacant ones smothered in dust, one a bedroom that did not show signs of current use, and one a spare room littered with heaps of newspapers and piles of cloth that looked like old drapes. Will thought this last room, lit by a gable window, might have been a sewing room for an earlier occupant of the house.

The window reminded him of the sound of breaking glass he had heard. Confident that no one was hiding in the upstairs rooms or had broken any windows there, he scuttled down the stairs. He checked the kitchen and dining room again and found them intact. Beyond the staircase, in the far right corner of the house, he located Donovan's bedroom.

The shade was pulled down on the only window, so the room had a dim, musty atmosphere. A bed, not very well made up, occupied the center of the room. To the left, next to the window, stood a chest of drawers with a comb, a brush, and a hand mirror sitting together; next to them was a tortoise-shell box that looked as if it might hold cuff links. Along the other wall sat a table and chair, the table covered with portfolios, papers, and envelopes. A jacket was draped across the back of the chair, and a heap of wrinkled clothes lay on the floor. Around to Will's right, in the corner of the room, stood a wooden wardrobe with the doors hanging open. By now Will could identify the distinct smell that lingered in the close living space of an old man.

Will backed out of the bedroom and went to the sitting room, which he had passed on the way in. There in the northeast corner, facing the porch, he found the broken window. On the floor beneath it he saw a hat tree that he imagined had been knocked over in a scuffle.

Blanche must have brought the girl this far, but where Donovan or the two of them had taken her from there was still a guess. Will tried again to place the noise he had heard from the front door, and again he thought of a stairway. He stood motionless and turned his ear toward the floor. This house sat high enough off the ground that it could easily have a basement or cellar. If Donovan was down there, he could hear all the footsteps from above, and if he had his white-handled revolver, he could make sure no one else down there made a peep.

Will sat in a chair and took off his boots. Carrying them in his left hand, he took soft, low steps to the center of the house. In the hallway, past the kitchen door but just before the bottom of the staircase, he saw something he had scarcely noticed before. A rug about three feet wide and six feet long lay on the floor.

Now on his hands and knees, he reached for the rug and pulled it toward him. After he had drawn it a couple of feet he thought he saw what he was looking for. Scooting back, he pulled the rug the rest of the way and then crawled forward on it so he could see the trapdoor. On the far end, inlaid in the dark lumber, he saw the square piece of hardware with the circular brass handle.

With his back to the kitchen wall, he sidestepped in his stocking feet until he reached the other end of the trapdoor. He sat on the floor and pulled on his boots, then stood up to take a couple of steady breaths. With his six-gun in his right hand, he leaned down and put his left hand on the brass ring. He pulled up, and the door, with a cord and pulley and counterweight and support arm, swung up and stayed in place.

He heard movement right away—footsteps, a muffled voice, and something like a wooden crate hitting the floor. A stairway made of rough lumber led down into the darkness, and he knew he would make a visible target for as long as it took him to go down. He also knew he couldn't jump, because the steps went past the opening of the hatchway. He took a breath, told himself this was it, and started down.

He took the steps as fast as he could, and as soon as he passed the edge of the hatchway, he crouched and jumped. Donovan must have been waiting for a full target and then must have taken a hurried shot, for the gun roared after Will had rolled into the darkness.

Up in a crouch, he could feel that this was a cellar, with a dirt floor. The place had an enclosed smell, cryptlike, but it was not damp. Nor was it as dark as it first seemed. A window on each side let in some light through opaque glass, and a bit more light came down through the trapdoor opening and spread beyond the stairs.

Still, he could not make out any human shapes, and the bulky square ones did not have distinct forms. An object next to him felt like a chair with a broken rung, and a lump lying on the floor beyond the staircase looked like a rolled-up rug. As with the room upstairs, he imagined that earlier occupants had used this area and had left a few things behind.

He was sure there was a lantern down here somewhere, but he was also sure that lighting one would give him the best possible opportunity of getting shot.

Glancing at the stairs, he tried to place himself in relation to the rest of the cellar. He had rolled to the right. If Donovan had been on the right side as well, he would have been close enough to try a second shot. That suggested to Will that Donovan was on the other side, probably behind some large object.

Will holstered his gun, moved to his right, and felt around. He laid his hand on a piece of lumber, not very splintery and sitting up on its edge. He gave it a shake, and he heard the rattle of glass. He froze, waiting to hear if anyone else moved, but the other party must have been holding still and listening as well. He reached past the piece of lumber, which he imagined to be the side of a crate, and he laid his hand on the dry, dirt-encrusted surface of an old bottle. It gave him an idea. Taking the bottle by the neck and holding it sideways, he flung it as hard as he could toward the other side of the cellar. He heard it bounce once, twice, and come to a stop. At almost the same moment, he heard a shuffling beyond the stairs and to his left.

Groping in the crate again, he found another bottle. This time he rose to a crouch, got good extension as he drew his arm back, and threw the bottle with much better force. It crashed on the far wall, and from the exclamation and muffled voice that followed, he had Donovan placed. Now he was going to have to go after him.

What he wanted was fire—some of Brad Way's shavings or some of that gasoline that Dunn spoke about. All he had was matches and cigarette papers. He crept back to the broken chair and felt it. The seat was solid wood, nothing that would ignite well at all.

Then he thought, the other two floors of this house were full of flammable material. All he had to do was get back up the stairs and down again.

Donovan must have been taken completely by surprise when Will bolted up the stairs, because nothing happened. Once he was out on top, Will left the door open so Donovan would not have a signal of when he was coming down again.

The stack of papers on the worktable in the bedroom made perfect fuel. Will twisted three to four sheets at a time into sticks until he had half a dozen. From a kerosene lamp he poured about a cup of liquid into a kitchen bowl, and then he dipped each of the sticks into the pool. Now he was ready. He was sure Donovan had been wondering and waiting all this time, but he still hoped for surprise.

He lit the first torch, and, reaching down between the slope of the stairway and the floor joist, he flung it in close to where he thought Donovan was hiding. Right away he heard movement and voices, and to take advantage of the moment he plunged down the stairs.

He heard stomping sounds as Donovan put out the fire. Using the turned-over chair as a shield for his flame, Will lit a second torch. Now he could see the center row of support posts and the two old dressers Donovan had been hiding behind. He lit a third torch off the second, tossed one around the far end of the barricade and one around the near end. Shadows and shapes were dancing, and the dangerous smell of open fire was filling the air. Will could hear Donovan cursing as he stomped his feet on the dirt floor to put out the flames.

Will lit two more torches and tossed them as he had tossed the previous two—one at the left end of the barrier and the other around the right end. He heard scuffling and Pearl's voice.

"Let go of me!"

It sounded as if Donovan was dragging her at the same time he was trying to snuff out the torches, and when he was at the far end by the head of the stairs, Will made a rush and pushed over the two dressers. The first one fell with a clean crash, and the second one clunked and then teetered on an open drawer. Now Donovan had less cover, and his route was blocked to get to the other flames. Light flickered and dark smoke floated as Donovan's head and upper body became visible. He was wearing a gray jacket and a white shirt, which contrasted with the dark-featured hostage he held with his left arm.

Will stood back with an unlit torch in one hand and his .45 in the other.

Donovan was not finished, though. With his arm around Pearl's neck and his white-handled pistol raised in front of his chin and pointed at her, he said, "Stop there, Dryden, or she gets it."

Pearl's eyes were fixed on Will, shining as the flames danced.

Will met her gaze, and as he let the unlit twist of paper fall from his hands, he said, "Drop."

"What?" said Donovan.

"I said, drop."

"I'm not dropping anything." He stood hunched and soft-bellied with his legs apart, but he seemed to have some strength left in his choke hold.

Again Will looked Pearl in the eyes, and she seemed to get the message. Her feet went out from under her, and she dropped straight down. Donovan lost his grasp and his balance, staggering forward so that he was standing over her as he fought not to fall. His gun hand waved until he came up straight, and as he brought the pistol around level toward his enemy, Will shot him high in the chest. He fell backward, dropping the white-handled revolver as his soft midsection reflected the glare of the torches.

Pearl was coming up onto her feet by the time Will reached her to give her a hand. As she brushed off her apron and dress, she looked past her shoulder at the man on the floor.

"He was a lot stronger than I thought."

"Surprised me, too. But he's done."

Her eyes met his. "Thank you for helping."

"You're welcome. I didn't have any choice at this point, but even if I had, I would have tried." He searched the shadows around them. "Blanche didn't come down here, did she?"

"No."

He wrinkled his nose. The smoke seemed to have thickened a great deal in the last minute or so. "Let's put out all these flames and get out of here. Go up where we can breathe some fresh air."

Chapter Fifteen

Blanche was sitting in the doorway of the cookshack, half in and half out of the shade, when Will and Pearl stepped out onto the porch of the ranch house. Will was glad to see her there, as he thought she might have gone back to Vetch's lair to wait with the rifle. As he and Pearl walked up to the place where she sat, he could see she didn't have much fight left in her. Her eyes had turned puffy and bloodshot, and her insolent demeanor had faded.

"Let's go sit in the bunkhouse," he said. "There's nothing to bother us there." Pointing with his thumb toward the cookshack, he turned to Pearl and said, "Things aren't very good in there."

As she nodded, she seemed to be absorbing the meaning.

Once in the bunkhouse, Blanche sat in the chair at the table and Pearl sat in the other. Will kept a lookout at the door. He was starting to worry about Jim Calvert and whether someone had gotten to him out on the range before he even made it to town. To take the edge off his waiting, Will undertook a conversation with Blanche.

"You still may not believe me," he said, "but the sheriff will come here. When he does, you can either hold out and make things hard, or you can tell what you know."

"I never did anything."

Will could see she still had some sass in her. "That may be for someone else to decide, but knowledge itself makes you an accomplice, and you helped hide and cover up any number of crimes."

"You'll have to prove my part in it."

"I won't. By now the sheriff knows where Bill Parnell is, though."

"Al didn't do that."

"Maybe not, but it's going to tie in with Ben Forrester. Anything you can tell will help put the blame on the right parties. The girl, for example. Marie."

"The old man did that. Choked her in his bedroom."

Will began to roll a cigarette. "It won't hurt you a bit to tell that. Where'd he put her?"

"Down in the cellar."

"Buried her there?"

"Had it done."

Will kept his eyes on the cigarette he was rolling. He thought that if he looked at Pearl he would lose his air of nonchalance, and he didn't want Blanche to know he cared about the missing girl. "Well, anything you can tell will make it go better on you."

"The old man's dead, isn't he?"

"Oh, yeah. Only one of us was goin' to come out of that dungeon alive, once we got to a certain point."

"Well, I've got the least pity for him."

Will lit his cigarette. "I can't say I disagree." At that moment he heard the *clop-clop* of horses, so he turned to the door and looked out. "Here's Jim Calvert," he said, "and it looks like he brought a woman with him."

Pearl and Blanche remained seated as Will stood in the doorway and watched the buckboard approach from the east. It was pulled by two horses, one a darker brown than the other. Calvert drove the rig into the yard, waved to Will, and pulled over by the bunkhouse. Mrs. Welles, sitting on the near side and squinting in the sun, smiled and gave a small wave. She had an uncertain look on her face but kept composed, and she looked businesslike in her same blue outfit.

Will stepped out of the bunkhouse and walked up to the wagon. "How do you do?" He tipped his hat.

"Well enough, thank you. I was reluctant to come, but Mr. Calvert prevailed." Her face showed unease. "I don't like confrontations, and I hope this one isn't too unpleasant."

"I can't predict that for you, but Mr. Vetch is beyond the point of giving anybody any trouble."

"You mean—"

Will motioned with his head. "He's in the little house over there. You don't have to look at him if you don't want to, but it might help to have an identification." He looked across at Calvert. "Is the sheriff coming?"

"A little later. He and a deputy went out to check on Bill Parnell first. Where are the others?"

Will turned his head and blew away smoke as he gave a backhand wave at the cookshack. "Ingram and Aden are in there, in the same condition as Al Vetch."

Calvert's eyes widened. "Both of 'em?"

"Nobody wanted to give me a choice today."

"How about the old man?"

Will pointed with his cigarette toward the ranch house. "He's in the cellar."

"I thought things were kinda quiet."

"They are now."

"Brad Way?"

"He's still out on his ride. I expect he'll come back in for dinner, wonderin' where his ridin' partner slipped off to."

"And Blanche?"

Will pointed backward with his thumb. "She and Pearl are in there."

Calvert nodded. "Less company."

"That's for sure." Will turned to the lady again. "Mrs. Welles, if we can, I'd like to clarify a couple of things before the sheriff gets here."

She put the back of her hand to her brow. "Out here?"

He noticed that her face had a flush to it, and he thought some of it might be from the sun. "We can go to the shade of the barn if you'd like."

"Let's do that."

Calvert pulled the team around as Will followed on foot. At the doorway he handed Mrs. Welles down, and the three of them went in to stand in the shade.

"Go ahead," she offered.

Will stepped on his cigarette to put it out of the way, and then he began. "I think when the sheriff leaves today, he'll take Blanche with him. I want to be able to give him everything I know, but I need to have things sorted out for myself first."

She closed her eyes and nodded.

"Mrs. Welles, did you know Bill Parnell?"

She hesitated with a small wringing of her hands. Then she met his eyes and said, "Yes. He came to see me. He was an associate of someone else I contacted, who declined the work. This man Bill Parnell came to me and said he might be able to find my, um, Al Vetch. He didn't tell me how he came about it, though

I would surmise that he had been given the name and was on the lookout."

"Probably something like that. I believe he came out here on another case and got onto Al Vetch sooner than I did. Thought he could work the two at once. I don't know if it would have helped me to know that, though I did ask."

Her strained expression made her seem tired, but her bluish gray eyes were sincere as she said, "I'm sorry I didn't tell you. He didn't report back, and I needed someone. I didn't want to discourage you."

"It's all right. I don't suppose he mentioned the other case to you, about a missing girl named Marie something. She used to work in the kitchen here."

"No, he didn't."

"Well, that was the other case he was working on, and I think he got it for that, although he could also have gotten it for asking about Al Vetch. I don't know. Blanche says Al didn't kill him, but that's not my main concern. It does look as if he did in a young fellow named Ben Forrester, though, who was also interested in finding out what happened to Marie, thanks to Bill Parnell." Will glanced at Calvert and then back at the lady. "As I told Jim earlier, I think Al was brought in here, through Blanche as you suggested, to work on some land deals. Then once he was here, Donovan got him to take care of a couple of people, maybe three if you count Parnell."

She gave a small shrug. "And as I also told you, I wouldn't put anything past him."

"With good reason." He brought his eyes to meet hers again. "I need to ask about another person. Did you know a man named Orry Dunn, who ran a way station?"

"Not directly. This man Bill Parnell was going to use him as a drop, as he called it."

"You mean, to leave messages."

"That, or mail to be sent on to me."

"Do you think Parnell ever mentioned Al Vetch to Dunn?"

She frowned for a second. "I don't think so. I believe he arranged this drop after he already thought he had Al located. I was waiting for a report, and when I didn't get one, I sent an inquiry to Mr. Dunn. He wrote back and said he thought Bill Parnell had left for the season."

Will flicked a glance at Calvert. "Just like Stegman did." Back to Mrs. Welles, he said, "A fellow who knew Dunn. And by the way, as you may know, Mr. Dunn was killed, also."

"I heard that, but I didn't hear why."

"Could be a couple of things. Someone thought he knew what Parnell was working on, or someone wanted to get his hands on a piece of land that Dunn owned. Either way, or both, it's a good bet that Al Vetch did that piece of work, and there's a witness out there who can probably confirm it."

Mrs. Welles let out a sigh. "I'm sorry to say that none of this shocks me. I'm sorry for these men who have died, but I'm not shocked at who might have done it."

"I'm not, either." Will took a breath and exhaled, preparing for the next part. "As for my work for you, I think we're square. I found Al Vetch, and you've already paid me."

"It seems as if I've put you through a great deal more trouble than that."

"The trouble came with it. Once I was in this mess, I had to get to the bottom of it." He smiled. "And besides, it wasn't all misery. I had the pleasure of knowing you, and I got the opportunity to make a friend here with Jim Calvert."

Their eyes met in understanding. She did not offer him more money, and he felt that she knew, as he did, that any additional payment could seem to be for the wrong thing, even though it saved her the great trouble of a divorce. He felt also that she understood he had no future with a woman whose money he had taken and whose husband he had killed.

"Thank you for your good work," she said, offering her hand and then smiling.

The familiar touch of her hand was reassuring, and he found it easy to smile in return. "As Jim would say, all work is good work. But there's some I hope I don't have to do again. Now if I can, I think before the sheriff comes I'll take care of one thing more." Touching his hat, he left Mrs. Welles with Jim Calvert and walked across the yard in the sunlight.

Pearl and Blanche were sitting in the same places as before, though Blanche looked more weary as she sat with her elbow on the table and her chin on her hand. Will stopped at the doorway.

"Pearl," he said, "I was wondering if we could talk about something while we have a few minutes."

She gave him a questioning look but got up and walked out of the bunkhouse. He noticed she had taken off her apron and held it folded between her arm and her ribs. She looked at once trimmer and less in bondage than before.

"What is it?" she said as she turned to keep the sun out of her eyes.

"If you come and wait at the other door, I'll go in and get your pistol for you."

She nodded and walked with him to the cookshack.

He made short work of fetching the black-handled .32 and giving it to her. She put it inside the folded apron.

"Is that it?" she asked, showing her clean, even teeth.

"Not quite. I wanted to get away from the others." He raised his eyes and found hers. "You can answer this any way you want," he began. "But you said you'd like to get out of here, and if you like, you can go with me. No obligations. If you want to go somewhere else, I can help you get there. Anyway, as soon as I talk to the sheriff, I'm done here."

She shrugged. "It looks like I'm done, too. But I don't have much money, and I'm on foot."

"Money doesn't matter very much. I've got enough to get by for a while, and you can ride Ben Forrester's buckskin. I don't think there should be a problem with that."

Her dark eyes held steady as she said, "It sounds like something I could do."

"Good. I'll make sure Jim thinks it's all right."

He walked her back to the door of the bunkhouse and then crossed to the barn. Catching Jim Calvert's eye, he said, "I need to fix the shoe on this horse I rode this morning. Can you give me a hand?"

"Sure." Calvert followed him around to the other side of the sorrel.

Will spoke in a low voice. "Say, you don't think there's anything wrong with Pearl taking Ben's horse when we're done here, do you?"

Calvert arched an eyebrow. "No, I'd say there isn't."

"Well, it's an idea. It looks as if she and I are both done here."

"So am I. I'm hittin' the trail as soon as I can."

Will tipped his hat back. "Thorns on the rose?"

Calvert pursed his lips and shook his head. "Not me. Not right now. But I'm not done thinkin' about it."

"You know what thinkin' does."

"I know. But I'm too old a fool to change."

Max Brand®

Luck

Pierre Ryder is not your average Jesuit missionary. He's able to ride the meanest horse, run for miles without tiring, and put a bullet in just about any target. But now he's on a mission of vengeance to find the man who killed his father. The journey will test his endurance to its utmost—and so will the extraordinary woman he meets along the way. Jacqueline "Jack" Boone has all the curves of a lady but can shoot better than most men. In the epic tradition of *Riders of the Purple Sage*, their story is one for the ages.

ISBN 13: 978-0-8439-5875-1

FIRST TIME IN PAPERBACK!

Max Brand®

"Brand practices his art to something like perfection." —*The New York Times*

Sequel to **LUCK**

CROSSROADS

"There's bad luck all around me."

Jacqueline "Jack" Boone couldn't say she didn't warn him. But Dix was a man who made his own luck. And he couldn't resist a beautiful woman who, according to tales told round the campfire, had bested one of the most notorious gunmen in decades. Except the people who were after Dix for a murder he didn't mean to commit are now after Jack too. Relentlessly stalked by a man known as El Tigre, the pair can only ride headlong into danger and hope that in the end their luck holds out.

ISBN 13: 978-0-8439-5876-8

ANDREW J. FENADY

Owen Wister Award-Winning Author of *Big Ike*

No mission is too dangerous as long as the cause—and the money—are right. Four soldiers of fortune, along with a beautiful woman, have crossed the Mexican border to dig up five million dollars in buried gold. But between the Trespassers and their treasure lie a merciless comanchero guerilla band, a tribe of hostile Yaqui Indians and Benito Juarez's army. It's a journey no one with any sense would hope to survive, or would even dare to try, except...

The Trespassers

Andrew J. Fenady is a Spur Award finalist and recipient of the prestigious Owen Wister Award for his lifelong contribution to Western literature, and the Golden Boot Award, in recognition of his contributions to the Western genre. He has written eleven novels and numerous screenplays, including the classic John Wayne film *Chisum*.

ISBN 13: 978-0-8439-6024-2

COTTON SMITH

"Cotton Smith is one of the finest of a new breed of writers of the American West."

—Don Coldsmith

Return of the Spirit Rider

In the booming town of Denver, saloon owner Vin Lockhart is known as a savvy businessman with a quick gun. But he will never forget that he was raised an Oglala Sioux. So when Vin's Oglala friends needed help dealing with untruthful, encroaching white men, he swore he would do what he could. His dramatic journey will include encounters with Wild Bill Hickok and Buffalo Bill Cody. But when an ambush leaves him on the brink of death, his only hope is what an old Oglala shaman taught him long ago.

"Cotton Smith is one of the best new authors out there."

—Steven Law, Read West

ISBN 13: 978-0-8439-5854-6

"When you think of the West, you think of Zane Grey." —*American Cowboy*

ZANE GREY

THE RESTORED, FULL-LENGTH NOVEL, IN PAPERBACK FOR THE FIRST TIME!

The Great Trek

Sterl Hazelton is no stranger to trouble. But the shooting that made him an outlaw was one he didn't do. Though it was his cousin who pulled the trigger, Sterl took the blame, and now he has to leave the country if he wants to stay healthy. Sterl and his loyal friend, Red Krehl, set out for the greatest adventure of their lives, signing on for a cattle drive across the vast northern desert of Australia to the gold fields of the Kimberley Mountains. But it seems no matter where Sterl goes, trouble is bound to follow!

"Grey stands alone in a class untouched by others." —*Tombstone Epitaph*

ISBN 13: 978-0-8439-6062-4

LOUIS L'AMOUR
TRAILING WEST

The Western stories of Louis L'Amour are loved the world over. His name has become synonymous with the West for millions of readers, as no other author has so brilliantly recreated that thrilling and unique era of American history. Here, collected together in paperback for the first time, are one of L'Amour's greatest novellas and three of his finest stories, all carefully restored to their original magazine publication versions.

The keystone of this collection, the novella *The Trail to Crazy Man*, features the courage and honor that characterize so much of L'Amour's best work. In it, Rafe Caradec heads out to Wyoming, determined to keep his word and protect the daughter of a dead friend from the man who wants to take her ranch—whether she wants his help or not. Each classic tale in this volume represents a doorway to the American West, a time of heroism and adventure, brought to life as only Louis L'Amour could do it!

ISBN 13: 978-0-8439-6067-9

ROBERT J. CONLEY

FIRST TIME IN PRINT!

No Need for a Gunfighter

"One of the most underrated and overlooked writers of our time, as well as the most skilled."
—Don Coldsmith, Author of the Spanish Bit Saga

BARJACK VS...EVERYBODY!

The town of Asininity didn't think they needed a tough-as-nails former gunfighter for a lawman anymore, so they tried—as nicely as they could—to fire Barjack. But Barjack likes the job, and he's not about to move on. With the dirt he knows about some pretty influential folks, there's no way he's leaving until he's damn good and ready. So it looks like it's the town versus the marshal in a fight to the finish... and neither side is going to play by the rules!

Conley is "in the ranks of N. Scott Momaday, Louise Erdrich, James Welch or W. P. Kinsella."
—*The Fort Worth Star-Telegram*

ISBN 13: 978-0-8439-6077-8

☐ **YES!**

Sign me up for the Leisure Western Book Club and send my FREE BOOKS! If I choose to stay in the club, I will pay only $14.00* each month, a savings of $9.96!

NAME: _____

ADDRESS: _____

TELEPHONE: _____

EMAIL: _____

☐ I want to pay by credit card.

☐ **VISA**   ☐ **MasterCard**   ☐ **DISCOVER**

ACCOUNT #: _____

EXPIRATION DATE: _____

SIGNATURE: _____

Mail this page along with $2.00 shipping and handling to:
Leisure Western Book Club
PO Box 6640
Wayne, PA 19087
Or fax (must include credit card information) to:
610-995-9274

You can also sign up online at **www.dorchesterpub.com**.

*Plus $2.00 for shipping. Offer open to residents of the U.S. and Canada only. Canadian residents please call 1-800-481-9191 for pricing information.

If under 18, a parent or guardian must sign. Terms, prices and conditions subject to change. Subscription subject to acceptance. Dorchester Publishing reserves the right to reject any order or cancel any subscription.